T0095695

WHEEL *of* FIRE

Also by Janet Nichols Lynch

My Beautiful Hippie

Racing California

Addicted to Her

Messed Up

Chest Pains

Peace is a Four-Letter Word

Where Words Leave Off Music Begins

Casey Wooster's Pet Care Service

Women Music Makers

American Music Makers

Janet Nichols Lynch

iUniverse books may be ordered through booksellers or by contacting:

iUniverse
1663 Liberty Drive
Bloomington, IN 47403
www.iuniverse.com
1-800-Authors (1-800-288-4677)

Summary: Living in California's rural San Joaquin Valley, seventeen-year-old Kori tries to free another teenage girl from a destructive cult, but falls under the spell of its charismatic leader, before attempting to rescue his followers from his deadly doomsday scheme.

ISBN: 978-1-4917-9104-2 (sc)
ISBN: 978-1-4917-9105-9 (e)

Library of Congress Control Number: 2016903501

Print information available on the last page.

To Laura Johnston Kohl

CHAPTER ONE

A pale stick figure of a girl shot across the dark street, matted hair flying, wild eyes glaring through the windshield. Officer Huerta swerved, slamming on the brakes. Kori felt the hideous thud in her bones. They swung open the doors and raced to the front of the cruiser. Kori braced herself for the shock of her first dead body.

No trace of the scrawny girl. Huerta squatted to look under the car. Nothing.

"Did…did we hit her?" Kori heard the trembling in her own voice.

"No." Huerta rubbed her hand over her short, spiky hair. "I…don't think so," she added, in her light Spanish accent.

"I felt the bump!"

Huerta walked to the back of the cruiser. "Hell, this is your bump." She kicked the right rear wheel, jammed against the curb, the tire deflated.

"She was inches away! I thought for sure…." Kori took a deep, shuddering breath.

"Get a grip, girl. We're all okay here."

"Yes, ma'am." Kori hoped she hadn't come off as panicky. As a high school senior in the Explorer program of the Goldhurst P.D., she was out to impress Officer Huerta, her mentor.

Officer Huerta radioed in to the station to say she'd be out of commission while she changed the tire. She popped the trunk, grabbed the jack, and swung the spare out with ease. She was a short, Hispanic woman in her thirties, built like a barrel, solid and strong. Kori had seen her tussle and cuff a perp twice her size.

A sudden gust of cold wind rattled dead leaves in the deserted street. Kori jerked her head around, searching for the vanished girl. The liquor store, pawnshop, and check-cashing center were closed and dimly lit, bars on the windows. Across the street, the municipal park was cast in shadows.

Kori ran her hand over the vehicle, feeling for dents, blood, or torn flesh, dreading a discovery. Nothing. "I don't believe it. She disappeared like she sprouted wings."

"Crazy girl. Goes by the name Flicker. Grab those flares and set them out."

"Wait, you know her?"

"Of her." Huerta fitted the jack beneath the car. "Lives out there with Wheel of Fire."

"She *does*? With that bunch of old hippies? But she didn't look much older then me, and—"

"Kori! The flares!"

"Yes, ma'am."

About a hundred feet behind the patrol car, Kori opened a flare, held the rod away from her body, and rubbed the button against the striking surface of the cap. The flame came to life with a sputter and a spray of molten potassium nitrate. Kori bent to position the flare on the road, then lit three others, blazing a diagonal trail back to the disabled cruiser. She bent over Huerta, her hands shoved uselessly in her back jean pockets. She didn't even know how to change a tire. "Need any help?" she asked tentatively.

"Naw, I'm good." Huerta shoved the spare in place and began tightening the lug nuts. "I'd just like to know what Wheelers are doing in town, running around in the dark."

Kori had been just a little girl when the Church of Wheel of Fire had arrived in Tule Valley and built their commune, Promisedland, out on Blue Ridge Road. Residents of Goldhurst got used to seeing Wheel members around town, shaggy and ragged, handing out their matchbooks and begging for donations. Her dad usually gave them a buck, telling her they would go hungry without it, but her mom pressed her lips firmly together and shook her head. "They have more money than they know what to do with," she claimed.

On dark, winter nights, when the Wheel's bonfires raged above the treetops and lit the sky for miles around, Kori would stand in the dirt road on her family's pomegranate ranch, wondering what was going on around that roaring fire, until visions of gyrating Satan worshippers caused her to sprint for the house as if evil spirits were clawing at her heels.

Kori rolled the damaged wheel to the rear of the cruiser and tried to hoist it into the open trunk. After her second try, Huerta nudged her aside, swung the wheel up and into the cavity with a swoop of a single, muscled arm.

Kori rounded her shoulders, feeling like a wimp. "What do they believe in, anyway?"

Huerta wiped her hands on a rag and slammed the trunk. "Don't know. They sure like fire. Isn't that the devil's home?"

Kori rubbed her arms. Talk of Satan creeped her out. When she was little, she had heard a minister preach, "Close your eyes and imagine the searing pain of hell fire and the stench of burning flesh, forever and ever." She had to sleep in her parents' room for weeks afterward. "Ma'am, do you believe…do you think there's a hell?"

"'Course there is, just like there's eternal salvation." Huerta pressed her fingertips against the gold cross she wore between her uniform shirt and bulletproof vest.

Kori mouth went dry; she tried to swallow. "Do you think the Wheel worships the devil?"

Gunfire *cracked.*

"Get down!" Huerta grabbed the back of Kori's jacket and yanked, causing her to fall on her butt, hitting the curb hard. She shoved Kori around the bumper to the passenger side of the car. Withdrawing her gun from its holster, she raised her head to peek over the hood. All was quiet, but the faint rustle of bushes across the street.

Huerta talked into the radio fastened to her shoulder, requesting back up. Goldhurst was a small town, and the other few officers were busy elsewhere. After several tense, silent moments, she put away her gun, duckwalked a few steps to the front passenger door, crawled over the seat and behind the wheel, and then motioned Kori into the car. Huerta started the engine, cranked the wheel in a sharp U-turn, and sped off with a screech of the tires.

"Do you think they were trying to kill her?" Kori blurted.

"Who's trying to kill who?"

"The Wheel trying to kill—what's-her-name? Flicker. That can't be her real name. What's her real name?"

"Why would the Wheel want to kill one of their own?"

"You saw how scared she was, running out in front of the cruiser like that. Maybe she was trying to get away from some bloody Wheel ritual."

Huerta grinned, her bared teeth shining white in the dim cab. "Maybe she was trying to get away *with* something, like cash."

"Like her freedom! I bet she was being held against her will and she escaped!"

Huerta nodded, her finger on her chin. "Maybe she's a human sacrifice. They give her a running start, then track her down and shoot her."

Kori's mouth flew open. "Oh, ma'am, you think so?"

Huerta threw her head back and erupted with her croaky laugh. "Death by starvation, if you ask me. Skeleton girl needs some eats."

Heat rose up Kori's nape. She hated it when Huerta played her like that, and she fell for it. "Chief Becker says they've got a whole *arsenal* of guns out there on Blue Ridge."

"No law says they can't. Law says they *can*."

"You don't think the shot had anything to do with Wheel girl? I know. It was probably the Ghouls and Freight Boyz fighting their meth war."

"We don't know nothing yet. How many times do I got to tell you? You need proof."

"Yes, ma'am." Kori wanted Huerta to think she would make an awesome detective some day, but when she got excited, she just jumped to conclusions.

The officer touched her shoulder. "Good job on the flares, Kori."

"Gee, thanks," she replied dejectedly.

Huerta braked in front of the Goldhurst police station and fluttered her hand.

"But Ma'am, I could help you find—"

"You know protocol, Kori." Whenever police officers went on a pursuit, they had to drop off any ride-alongs.

Kori pressed her lips against any further argument and bailed out. She watched Officer Huerta punch her lights as she sped back to the shooting scene. Stomping toward her truck, Kori kicked a rock so hard it hurt her toe. People were always leaving her behind. First her brother, Jared, then her dad. Her BFF, Bitsy, hardly had anything to do with her anymore, and her mom may as well be gone, the amount of time she was home. What did she have to look forward to now, but a cold, empty house?

She hoisted herself into her truck and sat staring out the windshield. The image of Flicker's pasty face floated before her, her wide, glassy eyes bulging in desperation. What would make her join the Wheel if her life didn't totally suck on the outside? Maybe everyone had let her down, too. Maybe she could use a friend.

Chapter Two

After the last bell, Kori drove out to Promisedland to do a little investigating on her own. She was in the wrong, breaking the first commandment of the Explorers by acting independently. If she got caught, she'd be in deep shit with Officer Huerta, but she just had to see if Flicker was okay.

After sighting her the previous night, Kori had gone home and looked up Wheel of Fire on Wikipedia. There was only a short entry with the whiskbroom symbol and the message, "This article may require cleanup." It said that the Wheel was founded in the late nineties by Vincent Dower, who preached a back-to-nature lifestyle for the new millennium. He and his wife, Sharon, began a commune outside of Casper, Wyoming, called Eden, in which they and like-minded residents grew their own food and provided their own power sources through wind and sun. All was not paradise, however. Neighbors objected to the Wheel's wild, all-night parties, when members allegedly danced nude around huge bonfires, accompanied by Wagnerian opera blasting from loudspeakers. One night Eden's main quarters caught fire and burned to the ground, yet no one was injured.

The following morning, Vincent Dower hiked alone with no provisions into the wilderness. After a few days, a search party was sent out, but found no trace of him. When he returned unharmed a week later, he claimed that he had communicated with God, who had commanded him to change his name to Promus and lead his followers to the Tule Valley in Tulare Country, California, to build a community on land donated by one of his followers.

Promisedland was located about eight miles east of Goldhurst, near the Sierra foothills. The valley was mostly barren land, dotted with a few ranches. Kori turned the bend and came upon a whole mob of strange figures, waving and bobbing in the wind. They appeared to be whittled out of wood, dressed up, and given such human expressions, it was as if the spirits of real people inhabited them. What were they? Scarecrows? Companions for lonelyhearts? Lifesized voodoo dolls that Wheel of Fire burned in satanic rituals? Really, her imagination was running crazy.

Next up was "Camp Rooster." On hilly terrain in front of a tumbledown house, were dozens of little fiberglass tents, a rooster residing in each one. "Why don't you arrest that guy?" Kori once had asked Officer Huerta, and she had replied, "Because raising roosters isn't against the law." "You know he's selling them to cock fight," Kori had argued, but Huerta replied, "Can't prove it by me."

About a quarter mile up the road was a dilapidated packinghouse, where the Goldhurst P.D. had found evidence of a meth lab. Both of the two local rival gangs, the Ghouls and the Freight Boyz, were suspected of using it, but neither had been caught at it. The only action there now was the rattle of dry weeds in the wind.

Kori arrived at the private gravel driveway leading into Promisedland. She parked on the shoulder across the road and cut the engine. There was no sign "Promisedland" or "Church of Wheel of Fire" on a mailbox. There was no mailbox. An electric fence guarded the perimeter of the property, and an iron gate was locked across the drive leading to a huge, two-story ranch house with wrought iron grills over the windows and the doors. Behind the main structure was a court of bungalows, a few out buildings, a large barn, and a multi car garage. Goats roamed in a pasture, horses swished their tails in a corral, and some chickens pecked the ground, but none of the residents were in sight. Although the Wheel aggressively proselytized, apparently no outsiders were allowed to drop in.

So much for your sleuthing, Detective Kori Lawton. It wasn't as easy as TV shows made it out to be. There was nothing she could do but head home. She started the truck, U-turned, and got back on the road. In a few minutes she smelled something burning. It wasn't a pleasant, smoky wood smell, but something nasty like gas or oil. Could it be coming from the Wheel's compound? Kori checked her rearview mirror. A pickup was bearing down on her bumper. Had a Wheel member caught her snooping and was now coming after her? If only she had her rifle hanging in the rear window, then the guy wouldn't be so eager to mess with her. Kori gripped the steering wheel tighter and accelerated.

The driver lay on his horn, stuck his arm out of the cab, and furiously waved her off the road. Oh, just some asshole with a bad case of road rage. Why didn't he just pass her? Kori pulled over, and the driver parked behind her. Uh-oh. Here she was stuck out on Blue Ridge Road alone, with this maniac.

He leaped out of his truck, a red cloth in his hand, and stalked toward her. He was just some kid she recognized from school, nothing threatening about him. She rolled down her window and called out, "Dude, what's your problem?"

He walked right by her and flung open the hood of her truck.

"Hey!" Kori slid off her seat and leaped to the ground. "What the fuck are you doing?"

He unsheathed the dipstick like a sword and pointed it at her. It was bone dry except a pinpoint of moisture at the tip. "You're driving this truck without oil. Can't you smell it burning?"

"Oh. I wondered what that was."

Intense sky-blue eyes peered from beneath tousled black hair. An unusual combination—her favorite, actually. "You don't deserve to drive such a fine classic if you can't take care of it."

Kori shrugged. The day her dad left for deployment, he had told her, "Take good care of Martha. She's the thing most precious to me." *It* was just a truck, an inanimate object. She had felt like asking her dad: what about *us*–me and Jared and Mom?

"What is it–a '94?" The dude looked over the engine and the front end. "No, a '95 F150 XLT Flareside. Right?"

"Whatever. It gets me from point A to point B."

"Not if you burn up the engine."

The guy looked so serious, Kori busted out a wide grin. He pressed his lips together to stop a smile. He was cute. Better than cute–*hot!* Not that she was in the market. He walked back to his own vehicle, reached in the bed, and came up with a can of oil and a spout, then returned to her truck to give it a long, thirsty drink.

"Thanks," said Kori.

"This one can isn't enough. You gotta take it in to an oil-change place. They give you a little sticker with a date on it to tell you when your oil needs changing, and if you just keep track of–"

"I got this!"

He looked around the empty terrain. "What are you doing way the fuck out here, anyways?"

"Looking around."

"Nothin' to see."

"I'm an Explorer with Goldhurst P.D., trying to investigate the Wheel," she humble bragged. "Know anything about them?"

He jabbed the air. "Stay away from those freaks. They'll get you!"

Kori had to take teasing from Officer Huerta, but not this guy. She laughed in his face.

"I mean it. They'll lure you in. Force you to believe their bull crap. Then you're stuck in there forever."

His tone unnerved her, but she straightened her spine and tilted her chin. "That isn't likely."

"It *is* likely." He gave a tense nod. "I know somebody they got."

"You do? Who? Is it a girl about our age? Goes by Flicker?"

"No." His upper torso plunged into the mouth of the truck. One moment they were having a conversation face-to-face, and the next it was face-to-ass. Which wasn't so bad in his case. He glanced back at her, his eyes narrowed. "I hate fucking Promus. He ruins peoples' lives."

Kori glanced over at the grillwork on the windows and the doors of the Promisedland ranch house. "Does he restrain his followers if they try to leave?"

"Doesn't have to. Holds them with his mind." He tapped his temple with his forefinger. "That's different, isn't it? You're Jared Lawton's sister."

"Yep. You a friend of his?"

"We did some of the same car shows. What's he doing now?"

"*Time*." Kori wasn't proud of Jared shut away in Corcoran Prison, but if anyone asked, she wasn't going to cover up.

The blue eyes popped wide. "Whoa. Was it that hit-and-run thing in the papers awhile back?"

Kori nodded. "Yeah. Who do you know in the Wheel?"

He slammed the hood of her truck. "Wanna go shooting sometime?"

"What makes you think I shoot?"

He gestured toward the gun rack in her rear window. "Me and my dad have some targets set up on our property."

Kori hadn't been shooting in months, not since her dad left. To shoot at the range under the age of eighteen, you had to be accompanied by a parent. She looked at the ground and back up at him. "I don't even know you."

A lock of wavy black hair dangled low on his brow. His lips tightened into an amused smirk. "Ah, come on. Your boyfriend won't mind."

Was he hitting on her? She honestly couldn't tell. "I'm pretty rusty."

"I'm no good at all."

She grinned at him over her shoulder as she opened her truck door.

He covered the few steps between them. "I'm Luke Jamison." He stuck out his hand. "Oh!" He made a move to wipe the grease off, but Kori shook firmly. She didn't want him thinking she was a girl who was squeamish about a little motor oil. Wait, she didn't care what he thought of her.

"You haven't told me about your friend." He looked confused, so she clarified. "The one in the Wheel."

The corners of his mouth tightened. "Forget I said anything. Take my advice and leave it alone."

Kori looked at the ground. How could she get him to confide in her?

He cupped her elbow, squeezed lightly. She started, glancing up at him.

"You haven't said you'll go shooting with me."

She climbed into her truck and started the engine. She tilted her head out of the open window. "All right."

He rolled sparkly blue eyes up to meet hers. "'Bye, Kori."

How'd he know her name? Through her mirror, she watched him amble back to his truck. Nice view. Nice indeedy.

CHAPTER THREE

Kori headed toward the back garage, her eyes cast down on the dirt road. She didn't like to see the splotchy, cracked pomegranates still hanging on the dry branches. In fact, they made her sick. Harvest used to be her favorite time of year. When she was younger, her dad had called her his little hired hand because she was out in the orchard all day, alongside the pickers. The pomegranates fit snugly in her hand like softballs. They bore a rich, rosy color. She loved watching the lug boxes fill up, then riding on the back of the tractor, swinging her legs, as her dad transferred the crop to the packing shed.

In the evenings, she would sit on his lap sharing a pomegranate with him, the juicy seeds glistening like rubies. She would ask him to tell her the story of Persephone, over and over, how the daughter of Zeus was abducted by Hades and cast into the underworld. There Persephone ate four pomegranate seeds, and her dad would place them in her palm—one, two, three, four—such a small amount of food, and yet it required Persephone to live four months of the year with Hades. "When Persephone was gone from her parents, her mother Demeter, the goddess of the harvest, mourned for her," her dad had explained. "Nothing grew in the earth during those months, so that's why we have winter." The story both thrilled and terrified Kori. She loved the change of the seasons, but worried about Persephone stuck in the underworld.

"Did she burn?" she fearfully had asked her dad.

"Oh, no. Hades was not like the Christian hell, just sad. Dark and sad."

Just sad now, not to have a harvest and not to have her dad around. She reached the back garage, turned the dial of the rusty padlock, and opened the double doors with a creak. No one went in there now. She switched on the light. Covered by a tarp was the Camaro Jared was refurbishing at the time of his arrest. The tractor, forklift, ladders, and lug boxes set useless. In the corner of the garage, Kori found what she was looking for: Jared's weights.

She used an old T-shirt to dust the cobwebs off the plates, bars, and bench. It was filthy work, and she wasn't looking forward to weight training alone in the cold, drafty garage, but being unable to lift that wheel into the trunk of Officer Huerta's cruiser was just too humiliating. If she were going to rustle the bad guys, she would have to build guns of steel. She looked around for the smallest plates and found two twenty-five pounders. Certainly, she could bench press fifty pounds. She slid the plates onto the bar balanced on the rack over the bench and secured them with clamps.

She started to lie down on the bench and felt her phone in her back pocket. She took it out, and set it at her feet, under the bench so that she wouldn't accidently step on it. She slid under the rack so that the bar was just above the tops of her breasts. She raised her arms and lifted the bar off the rack. Whoa, it was heavy! Too heavy! It wavered a moment in the air as she struggled to balance it, and then her arms collapsed. The bar fell against her chest with a painful thud, trapping her.

There was no use shouting for help; her mom couldn't hear her from the house even if she were home. Kori groped under the bench for her phone, thinking how ridiculous she would look to the officers answering the 9-1-1 call. Huerta would have a good chuckle. She searched frantically with clawed fingers and probing feet, but her phone was out of reach.

She was panting, sweating, her eyes tearing. She would have quite a bruise when she was released…if she were released. She couldn't panic now. She would just rest and take some deep breaths. How could the weight feel so fucking heavy? The plates, the bar, the clamps—they all added up. Jared had always lifted with a buddy. Now she knew why.

She squirmed and grunted, but no good. She was pinned. Didn't people conjure supernatural strength in dire times of stress? With a mighty heave, she lifted the weight up a few inches. Her arms trembled, and she was forced to set it down, this time beneath her breasts. She got the idea to roll the bar down her body, over her rib cage—*ow*!—across her abdomen—*oh*!—onto her thighs—*ouch*! She sat up, bumping her head on the rack before ducking under it, and then shoved the weight off the edge of the bench with a mighty clang.

Quaking with fear, rage, and exertion, she screamed to the rafters, "Somebody help me!"

That Saturday, she went shooting with Luke. She had found out that he was her age, but a year behind her in school. He spent a lot of his afternoons with the car club in auto shop, and he planned on majoring in Ag Mechanics in college. His family lived out in the country like hers, but on the opposite side of town. Driving over to the Jamison ranch, Kori felt excited about shooting some stuff up. She wore skinny jeans and her shiny new purple top under her Explorer's jacket. She'd even gone to the trouble of applying mascara and lip gloss. This was *not* a date, but she wanted to look good.

Her phone rang, but she didn't bother pulling over to answer it. Her mom was probably wondering why she hadn't vacuumed before she left home. Kori had to use her GPS to find the Jamison place, out on a narrow numbered road amid acres of walnuts. The lawn needed mowing, and there were so many tricycles, scooters, and toys scattered in the driveway, she worried she'd run over something. She knocked on the back screen door, but no one answered. There was a loud commotion in the kitchen, so she knocked again.

Luke yelled, "Come in!"

Kori passed through a back porch heaped with dirty laundry, boots and outerwear of all sizes, and more toys. In the kitchen, Luke was at the counter slicing bananas, while four little kids, the youngest in a highchair, ate lunch at the table.

"Hey, Kori." He glanced up at her, and then back down at his work. He didn't seem that happy to see her. "I tried calling you. I'm running late."

"It's all good." She had rushed to be on time.

"Have a seat."

Only two chairs were vacant. One was smeared with food gunk and the other was broken. Luke was arranging vanilla wafers and banana slices over pudding, a dessert Kori's grandma sometimes made. The front of his jeans was soaked with water from the sink.

"Pudding! Pudding! I want pudding!" chanted the older girl.

Luke worked faster. "Eat your lunch first, Annie."

"This mac and cheese has lumps in it," she said.

"It tastes like poop!" said the smaller boy.

"That isn't nice, Billy," said Luke.

The kids took up the chant, "Pudding! Pudding!"

Billy turned his bowl onto the table. "There, all gone."

The toddler in the high chair turned her bowl over her head.

"P-U! Someone needs changing!" exclaimed Annie.

"Is it Lizzie?" Luke asked.

"No, Connor," said Billy.

The oldest kid at the table, about eight or nine, bowed his head.

"Ah, hell," said Luke. "Go get changed, Con."

"I can't do it myself."

Luke addressed Kori without even looking her way. His face was dark, and he seemed totally pissed. "Guess we'll have to make it another day. I've got my hands full here."

"O-kay." It was an awkward moment. Kori could pitch in, at least clean up little Lizzie, but the mess was too big for her to get involved. She should head out, but she didn't feel like leaving either.

The screen door rattled, then there was a stamping of boots on the back porch. A man with a weathered face and bloodshot eyes entered the kitchen, shucking off his work gloves and cowboy hat.

"Dad-dy!" Billy and Annie lunged from the table and wrapped themselves around his legs, so that he stumbled to maintain his balance. He pressed his lips together in a weary half-smile.

"Luke won't give us pudding," complained Annie. "And Connor crapped his pants."

The older boy covered his face with his hands and scurried out of the room. Mr. Jamison released his kids from his legs, went to the sink to wash up, and then began serving the pudding, while Luke picked macaroni out of Lizzie's hair. Kori just stood there, feeling out of place.

"You kids going shooting?" asked Mr. Jamison.

"If it's okay," said Luke.

"Go on, I'll hold down the fort."

Luke looked at Kori, a hint of a smile forming. "I'll go see about Connor first, then we can book it."

She wouldn't help that spoiled brat. Obviously he was old enough to use the toilet and just wanted attention.

"I got it covered," said Mr. Jamison. "I want to have a talk with him." He turned to Kori. "Are you Bud Lawton's girl?"

"Yes, sir. How'd you know?"

"Recognized his truck outside. He and your mom and me all went to high school together. I heard he's stationed over in Iraq."

"Afghanistan."

Luke unlocked a gun rack in a kitchen closet and removed a rifle. He got ammunition from another locked cupboard above the refrigerator. He looked at Kori. "Let's go." Outside, he was totally different. He reached around her and lightly touched her waist. "Sorry for the wait. I was afraid I'd never get out of there."

"Wow, you sure have a lot of siblings."

"There's more. I've got two other sisters, but they live with our aunt."

"How come?"

He shrugged. "Couldn't take it anymore, I guess. You saw how it is." He thumped her shoulder with the back of his fingers. "Hey, you must be proud of your dad serving our country."

"That's not why he's there," Kori snapped. "Just an excuse to tear our family apart."

Luke pushed his tongue against his lower lip. "Uh…why's that?"

"First the cotton aphids got to the pomegranates, and then Jared got sent up. I guess he couldn't take it anymore either."

"Cotton aphids don't sound too serious."

"My dad gives up easy."

They looked at each other. Both of them had just blurted a lot of private stuff. Kori couldn't remember betraying her dad to anybody.

She got her rifle and ammo out of her truck, and they climbed into Luke's vehicle. They bounced along an unpaved road between the walnut orchards, nearly dark beneath the leafy canopy of trees. It was October, and the air was sharp with the scent of walnut husks. They broke out into an open field with a burst of sudden light that made Kori blink. When she leaped out of the truck, a crisp breeze hit her smack in the face. It was a fine day for shooting. She took out a tie and gathered her hair in a loose knot at her nape. It wasn't stylish, but she needed to see to shoot.

Kori and Luke set up cans on the fence posts and took alternating shots at them. She squeezed off one that blasted a soda can dead center.

"Good shot!" exclaimed Luke.

"Thanks, but I miss my Glock."

"You got a Glock? What model?"

"It was my dad's. He gave it to me before he left. Twenty-two." Kori extended her hand like she was holding a handgun. "A perfect fit."

"Forty-four caliber?"

"Uh-huh. It's just sitting around collecting dust until I can get a CCW permit." She would have to wait for her eighteenth birthday before she could obtain a carrying a concealed weapon permit. A strand of her hair blew loose and whipped across her face. She caught it, and tucked it behind her ear. "I'm a mess."

"You look good like that, your hair pulled away from your face. Let me take a picture." He withdrew his phone.

"Wait! Over here." Kori dashed to the fence, rested the sole of one boot against a post, cradled her rifle, and smiled.

Luke showed her the results. "Cool. I'll send it to you."

"Now you." Kori aimed straight at his face, crystal-blue eyes beneath rippling black waves.

They set up more cans for another round of shooting. "Hey, do you workout?" she asked.

"Nope."

"Would you like to start?"

"Nope."

"Would you workout with me?"

He flexed his bicep, striking a comic body builder's pose. "You think I'm weak?"

"No, me. I'm pathetic. If I'm gonna fight crime, I gotta get pumped." She jabbed him playfully in the ribs with her elbow. "Come on, do it with me. Your girlfriend won't mind."

They laughed together.

"I'll try," he said. "But I swear I hate it."

They improved in their second round of shooting. Kori got more hits than Luke, but he didn't seem to mind getting chicked like some guys.

"Whoa, you really are a good shot!" he said.

"Thanks. It runs in the family. Guess that's what got Jared into deep shit."

"He didn't shoot anybody."

"No, but that's what attracted the Ghouls. They kept coming around and coming around, telling Jared what he wanted to hear, until they finally jumped him in. He was out gangbanging the night of the hit-and-run. Ciclón Villadez was driving, and after he sped off, he made Jared switch places with him. There were witnesses, but the arresting cop fucked up the evidence."

"Bummer. What about an appeal?"

Kori shrugged. Jared's case was such a mess, she didn't like to talk about it.

"Tough luck. Everyone around here knows you don't argue with Ciclón and live."

"Luck has nothing to do with it! Jared screwed up his own life."

"You always see things black and white?" Luke asked gently.

"He tore our family apart!"

"I thought you said your dad did."

Kori looked down at her hands. They were shaking. She wouldn't be able to shoot straight now. She met Luke's eyes. "How do I stop being so angry?"

"You forgive," he said simply.

"Great. How do I do that?"

"I'm working on that myself. Maybe to forgive someone, you've got to understand why they acted the way they did."

"Are you thinking about your friend who joined the Wheel?"

"I never said it was a friend."

Kori raised an eyebrow. "An enemy?"

Luke's face clouded with abrupt rage. He spun around and stomped toward his truck.

Kori started after him. "Hey, wait! Where're you going?"

"It's getting too dark to shoot."

They had a good hour of light left, but Kori didn't argue. It was tense in the truck on their drive back. She thought to apologize, but she'd done nothing wrong except hit a nerve.

"Sorry," he mumbled.

"For what?"

"Being an asshole."

"You weren't. You just got all defensive about—"

"Hey, lemme tell you what happened in shop." Luke launched into a funny story, and by the time they arrived at his house, they were laughing together again.

Kori had had fun hanging out with Luke. He did seem moody, but she wasn't exactly Little Miss Sunshine herself. She was glad to find a workout buddy.

When she got home, she found Vaughn's tow truck in the driveway. "Shit," she muttered. Her mom could do way better than Vaughn Dirkman. He and her dad had been friends for years, and he had frequently dropped by their place unannounced, "underfoot," her dad called it. Since Bud Lawton had been deployed, Vaughn had been hanging around even more.

When Kori walked in the back door, her mom was cooking dinner. Dressed in a low-cut clingy blouse and tight, rhinestone-studded jeans, Cindy Lawton looked pretty hot for forty-something. Vaughn was in his work clothes, sitting at the kitchen table sucking on a beer. He nodded at Kori's rifle. "You better not be shooting in the dark."

"Sorry about the vacuuming," she said to her mom, pointedly ignoring him. "I'll get to it first thing tomorrow."

"No time like the present," drawled Vaughn. It was something a dad would say.

Kori glared at him. "You know, Vaughn, I think for once you're right." Running the vacuum, she would be able to drown him out.

They ate fried chicken, garlic mashed potatoes, and green bean *almondine*. Cindy was an awesome cook, but Vaughn's politics gave Kori heartburn. He tapped the *Goldhurst Sentinel* at his elbow. "Those good-for-nothing teachers are taking off the day before Thanksgiving."

"That's a furlough day," Kori said.

Vaughn screwed up his whiskered horse face. "A what?"

"The school district is broke so the teachers sold one day of their contract back. It's an unpaid day."

"Well, they shouldn't get paid if they don't work."

Kori hated herself for even trying to reason with him.

"Whatja shoot today?" he asked. "I didn't see you comin' in with no game."

"I missed."

"I could teach you a thing or two about shooting."

"No, thank you," Kori said emphatically.

As she was clearing the plates and Cindy was brewing the coffee, Vaughn went to the bathroom.

"You could be nicer to him," Cindy said quietly. "He's a good family friend."

"Oh, is that what you call it?" Kori could hear them having sex at night, even though Vaughn was never around in the morning, nor did he and Cindy touch one another in front of Kori or in public.

"You know your dad left me long before he left us," Cindy said.

"He didn't leave us. He's deployed. He'll be home for Christmas."

"Don't get your hopes up."

"Where else would he go on leave?"

Cindy didn't answer, but she must have had some hope of his returning. There must be some reason Kori's parents didn't get a divorce.

After she did the dishes, Kori escaped to her own room. That talk with Luke about forgiveness made her want to e-mail her dad. She wished she could hear his voice, but it was impossible for him to receive incoming calls from the United States. There was a satellite phone on his army base near Kabul, but he wasn't allowed to use it much. For every five or so of her e-mails, he would reply to one, with pretty much the same message: "Great to hear from you, Kori. Doing okay here. Love, Dad." She knew some of the maneuvers of his unit had to be kept secret, but really she had no idea what was going on with him, professionally or personally. Still she wasn't about to give up on her dear old dad.

In her e-mail, she wrote about going shooting with Luke and meeting his dad. She complained about Vaughn hanging around too much. "I think he's after Mom," she wrote, hoping that would get his butt home as soon as possible.

Chapter Four

Kori sat alone at a table on the patio of the new Chinese fast food place, China-To-Go. She had rebelled against Bitsy, who wanted their group to go to Taco Time to please Emma, the English foreign exchange student. Last week Bitsy had dissed the Explorers by calling it "the Girl Scouts," further proof that she and Kori were drifting apart.

Kori took her first bite of sweet and sour pork. Yuck! The meat was fatty, and the breading was soggy. She tried the chow mein. Double yuck. There were little bits of blue rubber bands chopped up with the vegetables. With a huff, she shoved the plate aside.

Across the street, a guy wearing oversized jeans and a flannel shirt, looking like a homeless dude without the shopping cart, scurried out of the main entrance of the hospital and was heading toward her. Not a guy—a skinny girl with stringy blond hair and a basket slung over her arm. It was *Flicker*! She was about to pass Kori, but stopped, eying her discarded food.

Kori pushed the plate an inch toward her, like trying to lure a wild animal. "Want this?"

"You're not gonna eat it?"

Kori shook her head. "I don't like it. Maybe you will."

Flicker glanced back toward the hospital. "I'm supposed be in the waiting room in case my friend needs me."

"Just have a bite or two."

She hesitated a moment, then hopped like a bird onto the bench across from Kori and set down her basket of matchbooks. She stared hungrily at the food. "I really shouldn't."

"I barely touched it. Oh! It has rubber bands mixed in it but–"

"I'm a raw-fooder."

"You don't eat cooked food? Not ever?"

Flicker reared her head back, glaring at Kori. "Sometimes. On special occasions."

"Then this is a special occasion, our meeting." She offered a friendly smile. "I'm Kori."

"Flicker."

"Hi." Kori handed her the plastic fork. "Dig in."

Flicker wolfed down huge bites, pushing aside the rubber band bits like they didn't bother her.

Kori had a hundred questions to ask her, but she didn't want to put her off. "Uh…you're a Wheel member, aren't you?"

"What would you know about it?"

Kori nodded toward her basket. "I've seen you guys around. A raw food diet is supposed to be super healthy, right?"

"It can kill you."

"Then why—"

"Fire is a gift. It shouldn't be taken for granted."

"Do you…uh...pray to…" Kori couldn't bring herself to say "the devil." It sounded cheesy, like a B movie. "Do you worship fire?"

Flicker's forehead bunched and her nostrils flared. "Really? Where do you townies get your ideas? We worship Jesus Christ, our Savior, like all Christians."

"Oh." Kori lifted one of the matchbooks out of the basket and read silently, "Armageddon, whose side will you take?" On the back were just three words: "Live! Fight! Fly!" She watched Flicker inhaling the food.

"What are you looking at? Do I got a rubber band stuck in my teeth?"

Kori laughed, and Flicker flashed a surprisingly sweet smile, the ends of her mouth turning straight up and the corners of her eyes crinkling. She was cute, despite her shabby appearance.

"I've heard of Armageddon, but I'm not sure what it is," admitted Kori.

"The final battle. God's followers fighting against Satan's minions to the bitter end." Her gray eyes seemed to bore right through Kori. "Whose side will *you* take?"

"Um…God's."

"Will you be ready to *fight* for God?"

"I'm a pretty good shot."

Flicker blinked. "Annie Oakley was a good shot."

Her comment was so unexpected that Kori chuckled.

"She was." Flicker nodded vigorously. "She was a real person."

"I know," said Kori. "I'm glad to see you're okay. I've been worried about you."

Flicker scrunched up her face and tilted her head. "Who, me? Didn't we just meet?"

"Yeah, but one night last week you darted in front of our car. It was a miracle you weren't hit."

She frowned. "You don't look like a cop."

"I'm not. Just an Explorer."

"You better not be exploring me. Cops are corrupt. They're the ones who commit most of the crimes, and then blame innocent people."

"Whoa, where'd you get that?"

"Promus. He says cops got no respect for privacy and freedom of religion."

Kori dared to ask, "Were you running from him that night?"

"Why would I?" Her face seemed to glow from within. "Promus is the best of all righteous men. He speaks with the angel."

"Angel?"

"St. Michael the Archangel."

Kori hoped her expression didn't appear judgmental. "Then who were you running from? You looked afraid."

Flicker's face slackened. She peered over her shoulder at the hospital. "I better get going."

"You can tell me."

"So you can tell the cops?" Just as Kori was certain she'd clammed up for good, Flickr whispered, "Ashe. I swiped some change from my collection can and bought fries. He caught me eating them and was gonna spank me."

Kori tried to act cool, but her hand shook with anger as she reached into her bag. She offered Flicker her Explorer business card. "Here's my cell. Just in case you, you know, ever need help."

"Help for what? It's you that needs help. You're the one who isn't saved."

"I'd like to be. I'd like to know more about Wheel of Fire. Can I attend one of your services?"

Flicker eyes narrowed. "It's not for you."

"What's wrong with me?"

"Look, uh…" Flicker glanced down at the card. "Kori, I'll e-mail you some information."

"Can't I come visit? I'm not a cop, really. Just a high school kid."

"No kids allowed. Promus can't have kids around."

"I'm almost eighteen."

"Too young."

"Don't whole families live with you?"

"There's some married people. If they have kids, relatives are raising them or they're in foster care." Flicker pointed her chin toward the hospital. "That's why Flame has to take care of her condition."

Her condition? Kori was shocked, but she tried not to show it. "Why no kids?"

"It's too late for more babies to be born. We're already in End Time, and kids don't reach the age of reason until they're seven."

"Where were *you* raised?" Kori asked.

"Our past lives don't matter. Only Promus. With him, I will never die."

Kori released her breath with a *ta*. "How are you going to manage that?"

"I'm going to *live* until Armageddon, *fight* against Satan in Promus's army, then *fly* straight into heaven." She raised her arms over her head. "Live! Fight! Fly! I would *hate* to die! Oh!" Her eyeballs darted wildly as she glanced behind her. She shoved the plate away, spat food beneath the table, and wiped her mouth on her sleeve. A stern young man with shaggy brown hair stalked toward them.

"There you are!" he muttered gruffly. "Flame's been asking for you!"

Flicker touched her fingertips to her lips and extended her palm toward the man.

"You may speak."

"It's too soon, Ashe."

"What'd you mean?"

She made the gesture again, hand to mouth.

"Yeah, yeah, go on."

"The second procedure. She must've not gotten her tubes tied."

Ashe's face softened. He had long lashes, full lips, and curly sideburns. He was almost beautiful when he calmed down. "Promus doesn't have to know," he stated quietly.

"But–"

"I didn't say to speak," he snapped. "That's the trouble with you, Flicker. You don't know when to shut up!"

"She can say anything she wants," Kori blurted.

Flicker touched Kori's arm and gave a quick shake of her head.

Ashe hoisted Flicker from the bench by her baggy shirt and hustled her toward the hospital.

Kori sat frozen, outraged by the man's treatment of Flicker. It confirmed her suspicions: the girl was in an awful place and needed help getting out. A full twenty minutes passed while she sat brooding. With a start, she glanced at her watch. If she didn't hurry, she'd be tardy for fifth period.

Driving back to school, Kori stopped at the light in front of the hospital. She spotted Flicker and Ashe in the parking lot. He was pushing a wheelchair, which held a woman with long, copper hair, who was slumped over, holding her gut, obviously in pain. At their orange Wheel of Fire van, Ashe scooped her out of the wheelchair. Her arms encircled his neck, and she pressed her face into his chest. Had Ashe also lost the hope of a child?

The car behind Kori honked. The light had changed. She tore her eyes from the Wheel members and drove on.

When Luke arrived for their workout session that afternoon, Kori met him at the double doors of the garage. She clapped his shoulders and bounced up and down on the balls of her feet. "I met Flicker today! I was at China-To-Go, which sucks by the way, and she just showed up at my table! Wait 'til I tell you the *radical* stuff she believes."

Luke cupped her elbows and smiled with his eyes. "Hold on, who's Flicker?"

"Wheel girl. The one I was stalking."

Luke mouth tightened. He sidestepped her into the garage, and began slamming around the new ten-pound plates she had purchased. She was about to ask why he was so pissed off, when he blurted, "I warned you to stay away from those crazies."

"She's not like the others! She's real young!" Kori lay on the bench, reached for the bar, and looked up pleadingly at Luke. "She needs a friend."

"Ready, go!"

Kori lifted the bar off the rack and pressed it to her chest. One, two, three times. On her fourth rep, she pushed the bar only halfway up and wavered. With a mighty grunt, she heaved the bar onto the rack.

"Good job." Luke loaded on more weight for his set.

"Her whole face got this eerie glow when she talked about Promus. It was creepy. You'll never guess where he gets his ideas."

"An angel," Luke said flatly. "He talks to an angel."

"Oh, wow, you know that part? Who would believe that? She totally needs rescuing."

Luke lay on the bench, making no move toward the weight. "Kori, you're not listening. You can't rescue her. She's stuck."

"But this other cult guy treated her like a dog. She was dressed like a bum. She ate that gross food like she was starving to death."

"She likes it that way. Anything Promus tells her to do—she fucking loves it." Luke sat up and looked up at Kori. "If he told them all to go eat poison and die, they would."

Kori batted the air and rolled her eyes.

"Oh, no? It's happened before. You know about the Peoples Temple, don't you?"

"I've heard the name."

"It was a cult in the seventies. Their leader Jim Jones took them into the jungle of Guyana to live, and then one day he told them to drink Kool-Aid laced with cyanide, and they did. Over nine hundred people died—men, women, and children—nearly everybody who was there."

Kori hugged herself, looked away from Luke's probing stare, then back again. "*Why*?"

"Their leader told them to. Jones thought the State Department was coming in to shut him down. He convinced his followers they'd have nothing to live for."

"You seem to know a lot about it."

Luke shoved the air with a raised palm. "Too much. I've watched and read about everything there is—the Moonies, the Children of God, David Koresh and the Branch Davidians—it's the same story. A charismatic leader brainwashes his people in the name of God. The more I find out, the more I realize there's nothing anyone can do about it." Gazing up at her, he gently pried her hands from her torso and held them. "There's nothing *you* can do for this Wheel chick."

Luke lay back again, while Kori took the spotter's position. She had been so certain Luke would be sympathetic toward Flicker since he also knew somebody trapped in the Wheel. Now she knew it was all on her.

That evening in her room, Kori dug the Wheel of Fire matchbook from the side pocket of her bag and typed its web address into her laptop. A sudden blast from outside caused her to jump. She clutched her throat, but it was only thunder. Heavy rain splattered against her window as she sat staring at the words "Contact Us." Finally she got the courage to click on it, and a form popped up. She typed her name, but skipped address and phone and just gave her e-mail. When she got to the box for age, she put eighteen, only fudging by a few months. In answer to "What are your interests?" She put "shooting" instead of "law enforcement." For the question "Why are you interested in Wheel of Fire?" she wrote that she had met Flicker, and she wanted to know more about it.

Kori didn't mention she was aiming to bust Flicker out. Her fingers hovered over the mouse, ready to hit the "submit" button when she heard Luke's stern voice grating in her memory, *"Stay away."*

Bullshit! Kori pressed her finger down. *Bam!* Wheel of Fire, your move.

Chapter Five

Sunday morning, Kori woke up to the delicious smell of brewing coffee. She pulled herself out of bed, put on her robe and slippers, and went to meet her mom in the kitchen. The week was so busy that Sunday morning was their time to catch up. Cindy was already dressed in slacks and a silk blouse, her hair and makeup done. She was in her "office," a section of the kitchen that held her desk and computer. Her actual place of business was downtown at Country Crown Realty.

"Going somewhere?" Kori poured coffee, added sugar and milk, and stirred.

"Over to the coast to look at some property. A guy in Pismo wants to put his place on our vacation rentals list."

"Pismo Beach? Lucky you."

Cindy smiled. "I'd invite you along, but, uh, Vaughn is coming."

"It's all good, Mom. I've got reading for AP Lit. I do have a favor to ask, though."

"Sure, Squirrel, what?" Cindy continued to peer into the computer and tap the keys.

In an e-mail, Flicker had invited Kori to a Saturday night Wheel service, but it sort of freaked her out to think about going into Promisedland alone, with all those bars on the doors and windows. "I heard of this church service thing," she said. "I want to check it out, and I want you to come with me."

"This morning?" Cindy glanced at her watch. "What church?"

"Not now. Next Saturday."

Cindy swiveled in her chair to look at Kori. "You're interested in the Seventh Day Adventists?"

"No, Mom. Uh…Wheel of Fire."

"Good God!" Cindy brought her hands to her head. "Whatever possessed you to have an interest in that bunch?"

"Just curious. When Officer Huerta and I were on patrol last week, we saw a Wheel girl running around town, and I just thought—"

Cindy was shaking her head. "I don't know what their leader tells them. He must use mind control."

Kori brought her coffee to the table. "What do you know about it?"

Cindy printed out something, logged off, and joined Kori at the table. "I showed the Hendricks place to some clients this week. Who do you think owns the title deed?"

Kori shrugged. "Old man Hendricks?"

"Church of Wheel of Fire. And Hendricks is not the first person to hand his property over to those crackpots. I've seen it before."

"Donate your whole *house* to a church? That's crazy."

"The Wheel owns Comstock Market, too. Sometimes I get this creepy feeling they're are taking over the whole town, like zombies."

Kori laughed uneasily. "Hardly! My friend told me there were sixty-three residents at Promisedland."

"So now's she's your *friend*?"

Kori nodded. Flicker had e-mailed that she was appointed Kori's designated "greeter" and that Kori should ask her any questions she had about the Wheel. Their exchanges had become more casual and chatty as the week progressed.

"Not all the Wheelers live out on Blue Ridge," said Cindy. "I know a lawyer and his wife who belongs. The Turners belong, you know."

"Mr. Turner, the *principal* at Polk Elementary?"

Cindy nodded. "Yep, and businessmen, teachers, and medical professionals. Don't think they're all a bunch of burnouts, Squirrel. There's some powerful attraction to that cult for ordinary people like you and me." She glanced at her watch again and went over to the sink to rinse out her coffee mug.

"Then let's see for ourselves what it's all about."

Cindy turned to face her daughter. "Kori, I don't think so. You're too susceptible."

That stung like a sudden slap on the face. "Susceptible? Do you mean weak? Gullible? Stupid?"

"Don't take it the wrong way. Ever since Jared…and your dad…I only mean you seem to be searching for something to hold on to. This whole Explorer thing, for instance."

"*What*?"

"Don't be offended. I just think you've gone overboard with Officer Huerta and riding around town in her cruiser playing cop."

"Gaining experience for my future career is going *overboard*?"

"You don't really want to be a police officer, Kori."

"Detective," she corrected her. "Criminologist."

"It's a rough, nasty job among a bunch of gangbangers and lowlifes. Didn't Jared's experience with the Ghouls teach you anything? You're not cut out for it."

"What *am* I cut out for?" Kori asked heatedly.

Cindy offered her one of her overly bright mom expressions and combed her fingers through Kori's hair. "Study what you like, honey. Go ahead and get your degree in criminology. Then you can get your teaching credential."

"Become a *teacher*! Stuck inside four walls for life? Where's the excitement in that?"

The sudden creak of the floorboards in the living room caused Kori to snap her head in that direction. She thought she and her mom were alone in the house, having a private conversation. Vaughn shuffled into the kitchen in low-slung sweatpants, his T-shirt pulled up as he scratched his disgusting, hairy potbelly. So now he was sleeping over!

"I could be a tow truck driver," Kori suggested, her tone thick with sarcasm. "That would make an awesome career goal."

"Ah, you couldn't handle it, girlie," said Vaughn. "There's a lot of skill involved in what I do."

Kori scraped back her chair, clutched her robe to her throat, and stomped toward her room.

That afternoon, Kori was on duty to clean out the dog cages at the Goldhurst Animal Shelter. It was next door to the police station; the town was small enough for animal control to fall under police jurisdiction. Kori had always wanted a dog, but because her mom was allergic, she had never been allowed. Since joining the Explorers, she had seen some sickening animal abuse, like the idiot who used fishing line and fishhooks in his dogs' mouths to secure them in his yard. Animal control confiscated the poor things, got them medical attention, and Kori had found good homes for them. In fact, she had placed at least a dozen rescue dogs with caring owners. Officer Huerta was no animal lover, and she appreciated Kori's help.

As they released the dogs one by one into the yard and hosed down their cages, Kori told Huerta about meeting Flicker. "She said the night we saw her, she was running away from a spanking. For eating french fries!" Kori took a deep, shuddering breath. "I want to rescue her."

"Stop right there, Kori. She's not one of your stray dogs."

"I know, but ma'am, I've been invited to one of the Wheel's services, and I want you to come with me."

"Ah, no."

Kori talked faster. "Aren't you the least bit curious what goes on inside that compound?"

Officer Huerta straightened, hands on hips. "They know exactly who I am, and they wouldn't welcome me with open arms. Nab me that pit, will ya?"

Kori smiled. "Why, ma'am, you're not afraid of a little pup, are you?"

"When pit bulls chomp down, they never let go."

"This one's got about all the pit bred out of him." Kori reached in the cage and scratched around his ears before coaxing the mutt out. "Go on, boy. Run around while I fix your pen up." Squirting the hose into the empty cage, Kori asked, "You don't care the Wheel is spanking Goldhurst citizens?"

"Folks can get spanked if they want. It's a free country."

"Wheel of Fire members are not free!"

"Over the years, there's been Wheel defectors, and they spill the beans. We have a pretty good idea what goes on in that compound, and as far as we know, it's all legal."

"But it's not right. Those poor people have no control over their own lives."

"Some folks like it that way. You know there're ex-cons who commit petty crimes just so they can get back in the slammer? They don't know what to do with themselves on the outside."

"Thief! Thief! Help! I been robbed!" A little Hispanic kid, about six, dashed up to the chain link fence, causing all the dogs to bark. "Hector stoled my rooster!"

"Who's Hector?" asked Officer Huerta, sauntering over to the gate.

"My friend. Well, he was my friend 'til he jacked my rooster."

Huerta pressed her knuckle to her mouth to suppress a smile. "How do you know your bird didn't just take a walk?"

"Cuz Hector tole me he wanted him, and he tole me to give him, and when I dint, my rooster was disappeared from my yard!"

Officer Huerta struggled to keep a straight face. "I think this is a job for Detective Kori here."

"Ma'am!" she exclaimed in surprise.

Clutching the mesh of the fence, the boy looked Kori down and up. "You don't look like no cop. Where's your gun?"

"I left it at home," she said truthfully. "What's your name?"

"Fernando."

"Well, Fernando, let's go have a talk with Hector." Kori let herself out the gate and locked it behind her. The boy led her down the street, up one block, and down another street. Soon they were crossing the pedestrian walkway over Highway 99, and descending into the East side, Ghoul territory, infested with drug dealers and car thieves. Her heart began to thump.

"Are you sure you're a cop?" Fernando asked again. "I don't see no badge."

Kori laughed. "I don't need no stinking badge."

"Are you going to arrest Hector?"

"Hmm…I want to talk to him first."

Fernando stood before a pink house obscured by thick cactuses. Kori's nape prickled. "What's Hector's last name?" she asked.

"Villadez."

Crap. Just what Kori suspected—Ciclón's house. "Tell Hector to come talk to me out here."

"Are you scared of gangbangers?"

"Cautious," Kori admitted.

Just then a kid about the size of Fernando bolted out of the house. He stopped short when he saw Kori and Fernando.

"I got the cops come to arrest you for jacking my rooster, Hector."

"You're trippin'. I dint steal your shit-pecking rooster."

"Can we take a look in your backyard?" Kori asked.

Hector narrowed his eyes at her. "You got a search warrant?"

"Nope."

"Then fuck you, pig. Fuck your pig badge, pig."

"She don't got no badge," said Fernando.

"Shit." Hector spit on the sidewalk. "You can't be no pig with no pig shit badge."

"You've got quite a potty mouth on you, don't you, Hector?" commented Kori.

Jesse Villadez came swaggering out the front door, his dreads tied up in a green handkerchief, the Ghouls' color. He was Kori's age. They had played dinosaurs together in Kindergarten, long before his brother got her brother sent up to Corcoran.

"Hey, Jesse," Kori said, trying to act cool. "I'm helping Fernando look for his rooster. He's afraid it might have flown into your guys' yard."

"Don't let her back there, *tío*," said Hector. "She's a pig."

Jesse laughed. If he didn't have about a dozen tats and wear gang colors, he'd actually be hot. "Naw, she ain't. She's a girl at my school. Let's have a look." He led us around the house through a side gate. There were hens scratching around the dirt and a couple of funny-looking Chihuahua mixes, a few torn up cars and a ton of car parts—probably stolen—but no rooster.

When they came around to the front again, Jesse asked, "You got any pit bulls down at the shelter? I want to get me a mean ole pit bull and fight him."

"Naw, I haven't seen any, but I'll keep my eyes open." She watched his face as she asked the next question. "Hey, you know anything about meth production out on Blue Ridge Road?"

He peered at her through half-lowered lids. That was one of the lying signs Officer Huerta had taught her. "At the old packinghouse? No way. It's too hot. The cops and the sheriff are always cruising the place. Unless, maybe the Wheel has a batch cookin'."

"I don't think they use."

"Who said anything about usin'? They gotta make money somehow to feed all them people slumming out there."

It was ludicrous that a church would be in the meth business, but Kori said, "Thanks, Jesse."

"Later." He placed his hands on his nephew's shoulders and steered him through the spiky cactuses toward the house.

Kori started to walk back to the station, her legs feeling like rubber.

Fernando fell in step with her. "Is that all you're gonna do?"

"That's all I can do."

"Get a warrant. Search Hector's house."

There would be plenty in the Villadez house that the Goldhurst police would be interested in, but probably not a rooster. "Sorry, Fernando."

At the entrance to the pedestrian overpass, the boy stopped and shouted after her, "I knew you couldn't do nothin' without no badge and no gun."

"I tried," Kori called back.

She returned to the animal shelter and reported back to Officer Huerta as they finished up the cages. About a half hour later, they heard frantic shrieks coming from the front of the station. "Get out! Get out!" It was the voice of Dorrie, the dispatcher on duty.

Officer Huerta dashed to the station's back door. She punched in the code on the keypad and burst into the hallway, Kori at her heels.

She drew her gun and commanded in a hushed, tense voice, "Stay behind me. And get down!"

Through the doorway at the end of the hall they could see into the lobby, where Fernando held his rooster upside down by its legs, the bird frantically flapping its massive wings.

"Officer Kori!" Fernando shouted down the hall. "I got my rooster from Hector! His *tío* made him give him back. He was hiding him in his mom's bedroom. I think he's been fighting him." Fernando lost his grip, and the rooster fluttered and scurried around the room. Dorrie grabbed a broom and batted it out the front door, yelling, "Shoo, shoo," as Fernando chased after him.

Officer Huerta bent over laughing so hard she nearly spilt her gut. "The only fight that bird's been in is with Dorrie!"

Chapter Six

Kori loaded her Glock, placed it in its carrying case, and headed toward the back door. Images of her shooting her way out of Promisedland caused her to smile to herself. She returned to her room, unloaded the gun, and locked it in her closet and the amno in a desk drawer. She got as far as her truck, before she retraced her steps, loaded the gun again, and removed it from its carrying case. She'd bring it, but leave it in the glove box.

Her mom was away for the weekend, visiting her friend Ashley in Fresno—or so she said. That afternoon, when Kori had gone beyond the pomegranate orchards for a walk, she had found Vaughn's truck parked in the packing shed. Her mom and Vaughn were sneaking around like teenagers. But Kori hadn't been honest with her mom either. She had told her she had plans to go to the movies with Bitsy and some of the other girls.

Driving over to Promisedland, Kori felt a little unnerved that no one knew where she would be. What could happen? She was just being paranoid. She had read an alarming account of a defector of the Moonies, a college student who had been invited to a single Moonie weekend seminar, which had led him to drop out of school, sign his car over to the Moonies, and marry a Moonie woman he hadn't met until his wedding day, along with thousands of other similar Moonie couples in a packed stadium. How could Reverend Moon, a little old Korean guy, seize control of so many people? Did Promus have that kind of power?

Kori arrived at Promisedland just as dusk fell, casting a hazy lavender glow over the open countryside. The gate was open, and some vehicles were turning down the gravel drive while others lined Blue Ridge Road. She didn't know when those gates would be locked again, so she chose to park on the outside of them. Kori relaxed a bit as she began walking in. If other ordinary-looking Goldhurst citizens felt safe here, so should she. The worst thing that could happen was that she'd get salmonella from raw eggs or bacteria from raw milk. She wouldn't eat a thing.

A rugged guy in jeans and a hoodie fell in step with her. "What are you doing here?" he muttered in a casual tone. "Just snooping around?"

"I'm curious," Kori admitted.

"About what?"

Kori glanced over at him. He was of medium height, late thirties, maybe forty. The shadow of his hood obscured his facial features except for dark, glittering eyes. A rifle dangled from his left forefinger hooked into the trigger guard. Kori hurried along. He lengthened his stride to keep up with her. She could feel his body heat, hear his breathing.

"You didn't answer my question."

Kori didn't want to talk to this creeper. He had a way of hitting on a girl that if she were to describe his words and actions later, others might say he meant nothing by them. "That's no way to hold a firearm," she snapped.

"It's not?" He seemed genuinely surprised. "I just hate guns. Scared of them."

Kori was forced to laugh. "Then why are you carrying one?"

"I know why you're here." He pressed his fingers to his brow. "You're seeking eternal salvation."

"Like sitting on a cloud and strumming a harp? Sounds boring."

"Smoke?" He produced a pack of Lucky Strikes, shaking it so that one cigarette extended toward her.

"I don't think you're allowed to smoke here."

"Hey, you're right. I won't be needing these." He threw the pack into the air and shot at it. The cigarettes dropped to the ground as the blast rang in her ears.

Kori jumped away from him, rubbing her ear. "Are you crazy?"

"Hell, this gun's no good. Here, see what's wrong with it." He handed her the rifle and tossed the cigarette pack so high, it cartwheeled in the air. "Shoot!"

Having no time to take careful aim, Kori blasted clean through the red target on the pack. Remnants of cellophane and tobacco fluttered around them.

"Bull's-eye," the man murmured, his eyes gleaming out of the hoodie. "I can see you like a challenge, and I like to make things happen. We'll get along fine." He abruptly turned off the drive and wandered into a grove of oak trees.

"Sir, your rifle!" Kori called after him. He ignored her as she stood staring after him. People walked by her, making an obviously wide berth, pitching disapproving looks at the rifle. She shuffled toward the large ranch house in a sort of daze.

"Woo-hoo, you're here!" Flicker dashed out to greet her, but halted, eyeing the rifle. "What's the gun for?"

"It's not mine! Some weirdo handed it to me, then just walked off!"

"We get all kinds." Flicker ran her fingers down a strand of Kori's hair. "Hey, you've got some little tan flakes in your hair. What is it?"

"Beats me," she said, shaking the flecks of tobacco out of her hair.

Flicker put her arm around her shoulders. "You look like you're dressed for a ski trip."

"I thought the service would be held outdoors around a bonfire."

"That's only for special occasions."

"I've got a lot to learn about Wheel of Fire."

"You can ask me anything."

"What's your real name?"

"Flicker." She smiled, the ends of her mouth turning up sweetly, the corners of her eyes crinkling.

"I read Promus's real name is Vincent Dower. How'd he come up with Promus?"

"The angel named him. It's short for Prometheus, the god who gave humans fire."

"That isn't in the Bible."

"So what? Hey, I have a solo tonight. I just love to sing!"

Flicker led Kori to the foyer. Not knowing what to do with the rifle, she leaned it against the wall and shed her outerwear. She picked up her purse, but Flicker said, "Leave it. It'll be safe here. You'll need your hands free for the service. Where's your phone?"

Kori withdrew it from her pants pocket.

"Turn it off and put it in your bag. Promus goes ballistic at the sight of a phone during a service."

Together they entered the great room. A roaring fire was lit in a huge stone fireplace, the firebox arching up five feet. Stuffed chairs and sofas were pushed back against the walls, and in the center of the vacuous room was a slowly revolving dais. Hanging from the ceiling was an enormous iron chandelier of electric candles, which cast flickering shadows over the walls.

The people greeted each other with hugs, clasped hands, and squeals of joy. Maybe some Wheelers were happy in Promisedland, something Kori hadn't considered.

"Which one's Promus?" Kori asked Flicker.

"He likes to make an entrance."

Kori met Glow, an aging woman, who swayed slightly as she stood. She had tiny, watery eyes and a web of red broken capillaries across her cheeks and nose. "I was a down-and-out drunk living in my car," she said. "Promus cured me. I haven't touched a drop since."

"Well, maybe one drop, Glow," said Flicker, smiling. "A drop or *two.*"

Glow's laugh erupted with raspy gurgles.

"Hey, Stix," Flicker called. "This is Kori."

A sugar-bowl-eared man with thick horned-rimmed glasses shook hands with Kori. He was dressed in jeans, a long-sleeved orange T-shirt, and a floor-length brown velvet cape. Stix said he had been working on his Ph.D. at UCLA in quantum physics when he first met Promus. "I was stuck on my dissertation. It was about the birth of a remote star you probably have never heard of. I realized what was missing in my equation." His rubbery face broke into a wide, expectant grin.

"What?" Kori asked.

"God! I chucked my whole Ph.D. It didn't matter anymore once I had found God."

Couldn't he have found God *and* continued his work in physics? Kori wondered.

"It's about that time." Stix approached a hanging gong, set it swinging, and tapped it softly with a mallet. Three hollow rumblings sounded to the rafters. The chandelier dimmed so that only the roaring flames in the fireplace lit the room. The people organized themselves into circles. Flicker had already explained to Kori that she had to stand in the largest one, called Outer Wheel, along with other guests and church members who didn't live at Promisedland. Flicker stood in Midwheel with the other residents.

The person next to Kori pressed his shoulder against hers, moving her over. The two circles were opening, creating an aisle for the small procession of the Inner Wheel members. Stix took the lead position of nine others who wore the same jeans, orange T-shirt, and brown cape as he did. Next came Ashe, who wore an orange cape and carried a cast iron staff diagonally across his chest. Behind him, second-to-last, was Flame, draped in a yellow cape, swinging a bronze container of smoking incense that clanked against its chain. The Inner Wheel members formed a small circle around the central dais.

At last came Promus. He was not tall, but had a striking carriage that commanded attention. His coarse, dark hair, parted in the middle, dangled like parentheses around his intense, nearly black eyes. He wore the same attire as the elite Inner Wheel members, except his cape was red and embellished with glittering ruby, emerald, and topaz gems. If they were real, the thing was worth a fortune. He stepped onto the dais and raised his arms. "Greetings, my sons and daughters, I bring you great joy," he proclaimed in a rich baritone.

A slow burn flushed Kor's face. It was *him*, the strange dude with the rifle! What had she said to him? Why had he singled her out?

"We are in End Time, our last days on earth," preached Promus. "Michael the Archangel has shown me horrifying visions of vile serpents writhing in the burning abyss of hell. Michael, the glorious prince of heaven, has instructed me to lead you, the faithful, into the fiery battle of Armageddon while Michael himself commands the angels." Promus grinned boyishly. "We're sorta like God's private army and air force."

"We're never gonna die!" someone yelled from Midwheel.

"Live! Fight! Fly!" others shouted in a rhythmic response, clapping their hands on "live," punching the air on "fight," and flapping their arms on "fly."

Promus beamed with satisfaction, but raised his palms to hush his followers. "All right, now. Listen. In End Time, you must be brave and strong. You must obey my every command," purred the smooth, hypnotic voice. "Satan and his minions are swirling about us at all hours, leading us into temptation. We are all sinners, aren't we?"

"Yes, Real Father!" responded the congregation.

"It won't be easy to defeat the fallen angel Lucifer, prince of darkness. Will you, my sons and daughters, be ready to follow me into fierce battle?"

"Yes, Real Father!"

Kori shifted from one leg to the other, feeling out of place. Did these people really believe this guy could lead them against Satan? He didn't even know how to handle a rifle.

Promus extended both arms, the jewels on his cape sparkling in the firelight. "Let us look forward to that final day when we may put the head of Satan under our boots, and cast him into the blazing inferno forever and ever, Amen."

At last! Didn't "Amen" mean the end? No, Promus wasn't finished yet.

"Spark and Blaze, step forward," he summoned sternly.

A young man and woman shuffled forward, stealing furtive glances at each other. She had a slender, turned-up nose, and he had a broad, blank face, fringed with curly brown hair.

"I'm aware of you creeping around at night, Spark. Where do you go?"

"To…to visit Blaze," she replied in a meek voice.

"To slip into his bed?"

She blushed magenta and hung her head.

"It's not her fault," said Blaze. "I invite her."

"Are you both so weak in spirit?" asked Promus. "Sneaking around, making your love a smutty, shameful thing. Why didn't you come to me?"

"We were afraid you'd separate us," admitted Blaze.

"Nonsense! I want you to be happy here in Promisedland." He twisted his hand and seemed to produce two gold bands out of the air. Oohs and ahs rose up from the congregation. Promus slipped the rings on Blaze's and Spark's fourth left fingers, perfect fits. "With the Wheel of Fire community as my witness, I pronounce you husband and wife. Go, live together in love and serve God."

Spark fell into Blaze's embrace, and they kissed as Flame and Ashe led the Wheelers in applause.

"Flicker, step forward!" Promus called, and when she stood before him, he scolded, "You've ate french fries? Don't I provide you here with all the nutritious food you need?"

"Yes, Real Father."

"As penance for your gluttony, you won't be singing for us tonight. A weakness for rich foods is a minor offense," Promus lectured calmly, "but you must be strong to serve in God's army. For an entire month, you must purge your diet of salt and sugar."

"Yes, Real Father." Flicker bowed her head, her wet cheeks glistening.

"Ah, come now, daughter, what's this?" Promus gently raised her chin with his fingertip and looked kindly into her eyes. "I forgive you. Be joyful and serve God."

Loud coughing erupted from the other side of Midwheel, and Promus turned his attention to a tired-looking woman with gray-streaked black hair rippling to her waist and striking blue eyes rolling in their sockets. She doubled over as spasms racked her body.

"Ember, step forward," Promus commanded.

She made no move toward him. His face tense with annoyance, he nodded at Ashe and Flame who escorted her to him, her steps hesitant and her face hardened.

Promus reached for the staff Ashe held, and with a flick of his hand it transformed into a lighted torch. "Ember, stand tall to be anointed by this holy fire."

The woman straightened her spine, rippling her flowing locks. Promus waved the torch over her head, coming so close that he nearly ignited her hair. "Suffer the pains of your weak mortal body no more. You are healed by the spirit of Michael."

Ember stopped coughing, but her chest convulsed and her eyes watered.

"Praise God, she is healed!" shouted Flame.

Ashe began to clap, and the other Wheelers joined in. As Ember returned to her position, Kori felt certain her coughing was only stifled—not healed.

"Kori Lawton, step forward," commanded Promus.

What could he want with her? Kori didn't even belong to his club. Flicker twisted around to smile at her, her eyes still red from crying. Kori gave her a quick shake of her head. Flicker took her hand and tried to lead her to Promus, but Kori stood her ground. Flicker continued to tug at her hand as titters erupted from the congregation. Kori relented only to avoid causing a scene.

Promus looked down at her from his dais, his black eyes glittering with condescending amusement. "Hello there, Kori Lawton. You're a good shot."

"I'm okay."

"No, you're good, better than good, when you can concentrate. Lately, though, you've been distracted, angry, hurt. I see that your aura is dark purple, surrounding you like a bruise." His intense stare shifted to her forehead as if he were reading her thoughts. "Your dad still loves you, just as much as you love him, and he wants to be with you. And don't worry about your brother. The courts will find Jared innocent eventually." He placed his hand on her head and murmured a blessing. "Smile, Kori Lawton. Your heart is filled with God."

Suddenly, Kori felt light and free. Promus held no power over her, and yet the crushing concern that she had about her dad and Jared was lifted from her chest. She was again standing in her place in the Outer Ring with no memory of walking there. The man next to her took her hand, and the woman on the other side of her did the same. The whole congregation had joined hands, as if Outer Wheel, Midwheel, and Inner Wheel were about to play a giant concentric game of Ring Around the Rosie.

"Come, holy spirit of Michael the Archangel," Promus chanted.

"Come, holy spirit of Michael the Archangel," his followers responded.

"Come, spirit of Michael."

"Come, spirit of Michael."

Dozens of times Promus proclaimed similar phrases and the people repeated him. The man to her right squeezed her hand, and Kori gave him a withering look. "Pass it on," he whispered. Apparently he wanted her to squeeze the hand of the woman on her left. What was this? Not Ring around the Rosie, but some other children's game?

The "squeeze," which Kori began to think of as the heartbeat of the Wheel, came around several more times. She began to anticipate it, and enjoyed it more each time. The pulse sped up. The woman next to her flicked her tongue in and out as she spewed gibberish. Tiny flames-- *tongues of fire*–appeared over the heads of some of the people, including Flicker. Fear closed over Kori's throat, and she couldn't breathe. She tried to free herself from the ring, but couldn't, as if the flesh of her hands had fused with the hands she held.

The lights came on. People released each other, only to hug with shouts of joy. Her cheeks flushed, her temples trickling sweat, Flicker asked Kori, "Did the spirit of Michael come to you?"

"The what? I don't…think so."

"Oh, you'd know for sure." Flicker's face was too bright, as if her skin were about to burst like overripe fruit. "He will come to you. He *will*!" She clasped Kori's hand. "Let's go eat. I'm starving!"

Kori was hungry, too. Maybe there was an apple or something she could have that wouldn't kill her. Entering the dining room, she was surprised to find a table the length of the room, loaded with roast turkey, mashed potatoes, side dishes, salads, and desserts.

As she heaped the delicious-looking food onto her plate, she turned to the people behind her, who happened to be Flame and Ashe. "Wow, this is amazing! You raised and prepared all this food yourselves?"

Flame gave her a confused look. "Where'd you get that idea?"

"Wiki," Kori admitted sheepishly. "I read you guys were self-sufficient at Eden."

Flame's tense expression eased into a smile. "Ah, Eden—what a blast. But self-sufficiency is hard work. We don't have time for that anymore."

"I thought you guys only ate raw food."

"Who told you that?" Flame glared at Flicker, who flushed in embarrassment.

"Some church members choose a vegan diet or raw food, but it's all voluntary." She continued to dog Flicker as she spoke to Kori. "I hope your greeter isn't painting a negative picture of us."

"Oh, no! It's all been very interesting so far," said Kori.

Flicker scurried ahead, skipping the desserts. Kori caught up with her and slipped into the seat she had saved her. Kori wanted to apologize for getting her in trouble with Flame, but there was no chance for a private moment. Every table was crowded and held a centerpiece of a bronze dish of fire. Flicker introduced Kori to the newlyweds, Spark and Blaze.

"I knew Real Father would take care of you guys," said Flicker. "Do you get your own bungalow?"

"Yep," said Blaze. "Number six. Right next to my parents. Hey, I wonder if my dad spoke—"

"—to Real Father about us," blurted Spark, finishing his sentence. "It doesn't matter." She wove her fingers between his. "We're married. We get to live together! Praise God!"

Two elderly women who sat across from Kori and Flicker were sisters, Roberta Frick and Rayann Malloy. Roberta had a round, sweet face like Mrs. Santa Claus. She seemed stronger than Rayann, who had a beak nose and a dowager's hump.

"What did you think of the service, Kori?" asked Roberta.

"She thought it was weird," said Flicker.

"I didn't say that!"

Flicker laughed, her mouth full of turkey and cranberry sauce.

"I've heard a lot of preachers interpret the Scriptures," said Roberta, "but I've never heard a man make as much sense as Promus."

"You really believe the world is going to end soon?" Kori asked her.

"Oh, it has to. There's so much evil now."

"Hasn't there always been evil in the world?" Kori argued.

"I just wish Promus wouldn't talk so much about fire," said Rayann, a vague look clouding her eyes. "When I was a girl our barn burned to the ground. I lost my favorite horse in that fire."

"Is that why you don't have fire names?" Kori asked.

"We haven't been given them," said Roberta. "It's an honor that Promus doesn't bestow on everybody."

Kori noticed Rayann's and Roberta's plates were heaped high with salad only, like a lot of the other residents. "Don't you like turkey?" she asked Roberta.

"Oh, this old system of mine couldn't digest meat," she said. "Not after all these years of rabbit food. It wouldn't even taste good." She slid a large chocolate chip cookie under Flicker's napkin.

"Roberta! You know I'm not allowed," said Flicker, eying the cookie.

"Fiddlesticks! Sugar is the food of angels. I'm sure Promus doesn't really mind."

Flicker looked around to see if she was being watched, then sneaked a bite of the cookie. After the elderly sisters left the table, Flicker asked Kori, "Do you have anymore questions?"

"Can I see your room?"

"It's private."

Kori cocked her head. "Just a peek?"

Flicker's eyes darted around her. She popped the last of her cookie in her mouth and brushed the crumbs from her fingers. "Follow me." She led Kori across the dining room and through a door in the back of the kitchen. They entered a dimly lit hall, lined with closed doors. "This is the men's quarters," Flicker whispered. "The women live on the second floor." They climbed the stairs. Loud classical music erupted from a room at the end of the hall. "That's Promus's room."

"You said the men live on the first floor."

"Not Promus."

"So the married people live on the second floor, too?" asked Kori.

Flicker shook her head. "A few have their own bungalows, but most of them live in the male and female dormitories."

"When would they get to have sex?"

"They don't. I mean, they can if they want, but Promus prefers his male followers to be celibate, and his female followers to be either celibate or…Holy Vessels."

Holy Vessels? Kori had an idea what that meant.

Flicker pushed open a door to reveal a dark room. "Oh, wow, I thought some of my roommates would be here. I better not get caught alone with you."

"What's so bad about that?"

"If I have something to say, it must be appropriate for the ears of the Wheel. We'll stay just a moment. Oh, why'd you let me eat that cookie?"

"Is Ashe going to beat you for that, too?"

"It's just a little spanking with a wooden paddle he has. All loving families discipline their children."

"You're not a child."

She sighed heavily. "Look, no one is forced to stay at Promisedland. If you're not happy here, Promus doesn't want you. This one guy Woody got spanked for smoking weed, and he booked right after that."

Instead of switching on the light, Flicker lit a fire dish on the nightstand. The room contained three bunk beds. "I know it seems crowded, but it's like having a sleepover with your friends every night. Here's my bunk. I love being on top where it's nice and warm. It's just hard getting up for Star Maneuvers."

"What's Star Maneuvers?" asked Kori.

"It's when we go outside for drills in the middle of the night."

"In the freezing cold? I'd hate that!"

"It's kind of exciting. Armageddon could happen at night. We gotta be ready anytime." Flicker hoisted herself up on the upper bunk and patted the place next to her. "Come on up."

Kori climbed up, even though she felt like a little kid, swinging her heels. "What's a Holy Vessel?"

"Uh, it's not something we tell newbies."

"Never mind, I get it. Promus is a player."

Flicker slapped her arm. "That's blasphemous!"

"Are you a Holy Vessel?"

"Oh, no! Promus doesn't choose a woman; a woman chooses him, by knocking on his door. He can reject her if he wants. I have the same dream over and over. He opens his door, sees me standing there, and slams it in my face." She shuddered. "Dreams can tell the future, you know."

"I think they reveal our worst fears. Why would he reject you?"

"I've been trying to get his attention for over a year. He just treats me like a naughty child." She stared at the floor, speaking in a tiny voice. "I know I'm not pretty." Flicker held up a swatch of her straw hair and frowned.

"Sure you are! You just need a good creme rinse."

"Yeah?" She looked hopeful.

"And a cute outfit. Don't they let you wear girl's clothes?"

"We just wear whatever we find in the closets. It's all community property."

"Then find a closet with some girl's clothes in it, preferably your size. How does Sharon feel about the Holy Vessel business?"

"Who?"

"Sharon Dower. Promus's wife."

"Oh, you mean Flame."

"*Flame*? She's okay with her husband having a harem?"

"You make it sound dirty. A lot of holy men in the Bible were polygamous."

Kori bumped shoulders with her and rolled her eyes up to hers. "You think Flame and Promus still get it on?"

Flicker hooted in shock. "Whoa, I wouldn't dare talk about any of this stuff with Wheelers."

"Where does Ashe sleep?"

"*Ashe*?" Flicker screwed her face into a sour look. "He gets special treatment. He's the only single guy who has a bungalow. I guess, cuz he's the Wheel's lawyer."

"Ashe is a *lawyer*?" Kori had to laugh. Why would a lawyer join a cult?

"And he monitors the surveillance equipment."

"What's he surveilling?" asked Kori.

"What are you doing in here?" A figure too dark to see appeared at the door. She flicked on the light.

"Oh, hi, Glow," Flicker said nervously, jumping down from the bunk. "I was just showing Kori our room."

Kori slipped to the floor, too. Glow shuffled up to her and poked her red nose up to her face so that Kori could smell beer on her breath. "What has she been telling you? Cult secrets? I thought I heard Ashe's name." The old lady laughed, phlegm catching in her throat.

"I didn't say anything I wasn't supposed to," Flicker said guiltily. "If you tell on me, I'll tell Ashe about that bottle I found under—"

"Relax," said Glow. "I'm not telling nobody nothin'." She jabbed Kori in the ribs with her forefinger. "You spending the night, girlfriend? It's past curfew. The gates are locked by now."

"Oh, no!" She sprinted out of the room and down the stairs to find the row of doors on the first floor all shut. She opened one to see a guy with his back to her, taking his pants off, revealing holey tidy-whities. She tried another door on the opposite side of the hall, but it was locked. By then, Flicker had caught up to her.

"How do I get out of here?" Kori asked frantically.

"This way."

Flicker opened a door that lead to the foyer. A single coat hung there, Kori's bag tossed in the corner. She hurriedly gathered her things. "Bye, Flicker."

"It was fun having you." She grasped Kori's wrist. "You'll come back, won't you?"

"I don't think so." Kori stepped toward the front door, but Flame suddenly appeared, blocking her way, arms crossed. "Where do you think you're going?"

"H-home. I have to go home."

"That makes it inconvenient for us. The gates are already locked. You can leave in the morning."

Trapped! Her worst nightmare! "No! I can't." Panic rose in Kori's voice. "My mother's expecting me."

Flame's lips pushed into a bitter smile. "You should have thought about that before you went prowling around *our* home after curfew."

Loud pounding from outside caused the door to shake on its hinges.

"Open up, Ashe!" a man called out. "Look who I found snooping around again, looking for his mommy!"

Another male voice shouted, "Let me go, you fucker, let me go!"

"Hey, Ashe, want me to teach him a lesson he won't forget so easy this time?"

"I'm not trying to see my mother! I'm picking up a friend!"

Flame eyes widened. She turned, unlocked the front door, and opened it a crack. Kori gripped the door, pulled it open, and wedged her body through, her adrenaline coursing through her body to fuel a sprint all the way to her truck. But the spectacle she encountered caused her to freeze. A guy in his late twenties with skull-and-bone ear spacers and rotten teeth stood behind his struggling captive, securing him with a chokehold.

"Luke!" Kori exclaimed.

"There she is!" he said.

Flame slapped his captor's arm. "Scorch, you idiot. Let him go!"

The goon dropped his arms to his sides and peered sheepishly into Flame's face. "Ashe told me if I ever saw this dude on our property again—"

"Never mind!" Flame interrupted. "Scorch, please escort our *guests* to the gate and see that they get off safely."

Kori and Luke walked side by side down the dirt road, Scorch following close behind. "Your *mother*?" she asked through clenched teeth. "That's who you know in there?"

"Not now," Luke whispered urgently.

Scorch unlocked the gate and swung it open. Across the highway was Luke's truck parked in front of Kori's. Each of them got into their vehicles, and drove off, Kori following Luke, as Scorch looked on. About a mile down the road, Luke put on his signal and pulled onto the shoulder; Kori parked behind him. He leaped out of his truck and dashed toward her. She opened her door, and he pulled her out into a crushing embrace. He held her head in his hands, kissed her hair, her eyelids, her cheeks. She offered her mouth to him, and he took it, drinking long and deep their first kiss.

His body trembled. "I thought I'd lost you! I thought they got you, too!"

"I just went to the service. How did you know where to find me?"

"I wanted to hang out, but you didn't answer your phone. I drove by your house, but no one seemed to be home. Heading back to my place, I spotted your truck. All the visitors came streaming out of Promisedland except you!"

A blast of wind whipped around them, and Kori shivered. "Let's get into my truck." She climbed into the driver's seat, but before she could unlock the passenger's door, Luke slid in.

"You shouldn't leave your truck unlocked out on this desolate road."

"I didn't."

"The passenger's side, you did."

"Luke, I didn't!" She fumbled to get the glove box open. Her Glock was tucked away there, just as she left it. She pressed her palm to her chest and heaved a sigh.

"You're packing without a CCW *and* leaving your truck unlocked?"

"Listen, will you? They told me to leave my purse in the foyer. Someone must've taken my keys and gone out to my truck. What could they want?"

"Information. That's how they *get* people. You're lucky they didn't take your gun."

"Thank God you showed up! They were going to make me spend the night!"

He actually laughed. "They were just trying to scare you away."

"I thought they try to get people *in.*"

"Trust me. They don't want you. And they don't want you hanging around your friend Flicker either. You don't fit the profile."

"Why not?"

Luke ticked the reasons off on his fingers. "A high school kid bound for college, living with a mom who loves you and keeps track of you, an interest in law enforcement, an affiliation with the local police. Someone with a life."

"Like a wife and mother of seven kids?"

Luke's sigh erupted like a shudder. "No one can understand it. My mom split soon after Lizzie was born. Just walked out of the house and drove off. When Connor got off the bus that afternoon, he found Lizzie in her crib screaming her head off and Billy and Annie running around the backyard with no one watching them."

"Was she super into God?"

Luke shrugged. "She read the Bible, and we all went to church, but it was Valley Community, and that's pretty chill. Dad went over to Promisedland to visit her a few times, but eventually Promus forced her to take the Shunning Vow."

Kori winced. "Is that as bad as it sounds?"

Luke nodded. "Promus orders his followers to separate themselves from family or friends who are critical of the Wheel. We haven't seen or heard from Mom in nearly two years."

"I wonder if I saw your mom tonight, not knowing who she was. What's her name?"

"Maureen. In there, they call her Ember."

Kori gasped. "I did see her. She's sick. She has a really bad cough. It sounded like she needs a doctor."

Luke shook his head. "Promus won't want to pay for it."

"He married two people. He did a sort of magic trick." She described Blaze and Spark's "wedding."

"That's cheap. Any third-grader can learn to produce rings out of his sleeve."

"Those two are lucky they get to live together. Most married couples in Promisedland live separately, men on the bottom floor, women upstairs."

Luke nodded. "Of course. That way a spouse is not the most important person in a Wheeler's life. Promus is."

"Oh, he's full of himself." Kori still couldn't explain to herself how she had taken that shot of the cigarette pack. She was ashamed to admit it to Luke. "Poor Flicker. She's got nobody."

"You know that for a fact?"

"I don't know a thing about her. If I could find out her identity, I could contact her family. At least let them know where she is."

"You think they don't know?"

She shrugged, smiling ruefully.

"A lot of Wheelers come from the valley. You could start by searching through high school yearbooks."

"Missing Persons!" Kori exclaimed. "I can check those files at the P.D."

"You're the detective, babe, you'll figure it out."

Babe. Kori and Luke were a couple now, not just workout buddies.

So much had happened in one night, Kori's head was spinning. She was home before she realized she had driven there. She made hot cocoa, got ready for bed, but she knew she would never get to sleep.

She thought of that stuff Promus had said about her dad coming home and Jared getting released from prison. She didn't really believe he could predict the future, but what was the harm in her envisioning her whole family gathered around the Christmas tree together?

She climbed into bed, switched off the light, and lay staring at the ceiling. Suddenly, she remembered her phone was off. Ha! Something had happened to her that was actually more interesting than checking her phone.

When she turned it on, there was a missed call. It was from her dad.

Chapter Seven

There were about twenty-five thousand individuals in the missing persons system from California alone, but age, gender, and date of disappearance narrowed Kori's search. Some of the girls had heavy makeup, tats and piercings, hair hanging in their faces, and a look about them that said, "Leave me alone. I don't want to be found." Others were ordinary, smiling girls, all fixed up for school picture day. One of them, a Stephanie Welch from Chico, looked like Flicker, but she'd been missing eight years. Kori's family had a tough time coping with Jared in prison, but at least they knew he was getting decent food and shelter. At least they knew where he was. This girl's loved ones had to wonder every day if she was being held captive, raped, and tortured, and they might never know what happened to her.

Kori continued to scan the missing persons' photographs on a computer in Officer Huerta's office. Another girl, Chelsea Cunningham, missing from Marina Del Rey, had Flicker's distinctive smile, with the ends of her mouth turned up a centimeter or so and crinkles at the corners of her eyes. She had been missing since a year ago spring—eighteen months—which could be right for Flicker's timeline, but this girl was too young, only nineteen, while Flicker had to be at least twenty.

Huerta peered over Kori's shoulder. "Lose somebody?"

"I'm trying to find out more about Flicker."

"Her again. Do you know for a fact she's a missing person?"

Kori shrugged. "Just a feeling. Look at this girl. You think it's her?"

Officer Huerta squinted at the photo. The girl's blond hair was styled, her makeup carefully applied, and she wore a white lacy blouse. "Nope. That girl has a life."

Kori pushed the bar with all her might, sweating and trembling with the effort. With a final heave and a yelp, she racked the weight. "I did it! I did it! A hundred pounds!" She sat up and wiped her face with a towel.

"Congratulations, babe." Luke bent over for a quick kiss, before loading the bar with more weight for his set. "Wanna see a movie Saturday night?"

"Uh…no. I've got plans."

"Okay." Luke lay on the bench. There was a tension in the silence between them. He hadn't asked Kori what her plans were, but it was obvious he expected her to tell him. He was right, she knew. There was no point in having a relationship if they were going to keep secrets from one another. Luke reached for the bar, then dropped his arms and sat up. "You know what? I really don't feel like doing this today."

Kori placed her hands on his shoulders and looked into his eyes. "I've decided to go back."

"*What*?" He pushed her hands away and stood up.

"I wasn't going to, but Flicker keeps e-mailing me to come back. She seems lonely, and, oh, Luke, I have an idea! I want to try something with your mom."

He sighed deeply and dropped his head, running his hand through his hair.

"Look." Kori reached for her jacket and withdrew a photo of Luke, the one she had taken of him the first time they had gone shooting together. "I want to give this to your mom. I want her to remember the family she left behind."

"I know you're trying to help, babe. You're sweet, but naive. The Wheel doesn't tolerate casual observers. They're either going to pressure you to join or force you to stay away."

"Just one more time, Luke." She held up the photo to him. "I just want to deliver this beautiful boy to his mom. That's it, I promise."

Kori's second trip to Promisedland felt anticlimactic, and the service was totally boring. As Promus preached, his black glittering eyes passed over her as if he had no interest in her. She was relieved. She often thought of shooting off the rifle in his presence, when she had no intention of doing so. His prediction that her dad was coming home and Jared was getting off was only his exploiting her wishful thinking. Promus didn't know shit. He was just a weird, creepy egomaniac, who was able to fool a lot of people. Not her.

As the Wheelers repeated the robotic responses to the St. Michael litany, Kori had a chance to observe Luke's mom. Her cough seemed better, but she often clenched her throat, her face flushed and her eyes watering. Sometimes she didn't bother voicing the responses with the rest of the congregation, and at the end of the summoning of the spirit of St. Michael, she didn't have that sweaty glow the other Wheelers did. Clearly she wasn't as into it as they were, but maybe that was because she was so sick.

After the service, when Kori stood in line with Flicker at the feast, Flame came up to her and said, "Oh, you're back. You're becoming a member?"

"Oh, I…um…I don't think so."

"Then why are you here? Out for the free meal? Really, we can't afford to feed outsiders."

"Give her a chance," Flicker piped up. "She hasn't made up her mind. It's a lot to take in. I'm trying to explain it to her."

"Just see that you don't forget the Rule of the Four Horsemen," said Flame, causing Flicker to blush and drop her chin.

When Flame walked away, Kori asked, "Four Horsemen?"

"Wheel members have to always gather in groups of four or more. Flame found out we spent some time alone in my room."

"But we didn't do anything wrong."

"Yeah, we did. We broke the rule. We ended up talking about things we shouldn't have."

As Kori and Flicker ate their meal, Ember served coffee and removed empty plates as the diners finished. Kori tilted her head in her direction. "Is that her job?"

"No, her job is lead gatherer, getting all the food we eat," explained Flicker, "but she never seems to stop working. She's like a mom taking care of a big family."

"Uh-huh." Kori thought of Luke, trying to feed all his whining siblings lunch in the Jamison's messy kitchen. As Ember carried a pile of dirty dishes toward the kitchen, Kori got up to follow her.

Flicker touched her wrist. "Where are you going?"

"Back to the dessert table."

"Oh, they don't like you to have seconds. It's gluttony, and well, it costs too much."

"I just want to look. I love looking at desserts."

Flicker's brow creased. With her penance of no sugar, she couldn't be seen near the desserts.

"Finish your salad," Kori said. "I'll be right back."

Kori gathered a few plates off some tables and brought them into the kitchen. Ember had retreated to a stool in the corner of the room and was flipping through a worn Bible.

Kori set down her load with a clatter to get her attention.

Ember looked up. "Oh, you don't have to do that. You're our guest."

"I want to. I much rather do something than just sit around."

Ember smiled with her crystal blue eyes. "That's how I am. This is your second time here, isn't it? Are you thinking of joining us?"

"Uh, well, I couldn't live here. I'm still in high school. I live at home with my mom and…" Kori grinned wide. "I've got a boyfriend who wouldn't be into this."

"Ah, I can tell by the look on your face he's someone special."

"Yeah. We're kinda new but–hey, I'll show you a picture." Kori's fingers trembled when she withdrew the photo of Luke from her back jean's pocket and handed it to Ember.

She reared back, gazing at the photograph a long moment. "He's very handsome, but he needs a haircut." She tried to return the photo.

"You keep it."

"Why would I want…? How did you find me?" she whispered.

Steadily, she held Ember's gaze. "Luke told me you were here. He has your eyes."

She pushed the photo into Kori's hand and pressed her fingers to her heart. "Luke is here, with my husband and all my children."

"Do you know that Connor poops his pants?" Kori blurted.

Ember's brow creased with concern. "Certainly his dad is getting him help."

"I don't know about that. Luke thinks it's Connor's way of saying he wants his mom to come home and take care of him." Kori's voice had developed a scolding tone she hadn't intended.

"They're better off without me."

"What's that supposed to mean?"

"Ember," someone called from the entry of the kitchen, "the coffee urn is empty."

"I'll be right there." She set her Bible face down on the counter to mark her place and slid off the stool. She twisted her head to offer Kori one last forlorn look, then rushed out of the kitchen. Kori picked up the Bible and slipped Luke's photo inside—a surprise bookmark.

As Kori exited the kitchen, Flicker rushed up to her. "There you are! I thought I'd lost you!"

"I was just talking to Ember. I better get going."

"You can't stay awhile longer? I was going to introduce you to some other people."

"Flame doesn't like me here."

Flicker leaned into her ear and whispered, "Flame doesn't like pretty girls."

CHAPTER EIGHT

Kori was surprised to receive a text from Flicker, inviting her to a members-only Wednesday night Wheel of Fire service. "I'm not a member," she replied.

"I'm sponsoring you," Flicker wrote back. "You're required to attend on a Wednesday before you come on another Saturday."

Kori hadn't found out anything about Flicker's identity, and Luke's mom hadn't tried to contact her family. In her mind, the Case of the Wheel of Fire was closed. "I won't be coming to anymore Saturdays," she replied.

"Try a Wednesday. It's totally different."

Kori reluctantly accepted the invitation. She was curious, and she wanted to see Flicker again. She decided not to tell Luke or her mom where she was going, allowing them to assume that she was attending her usual Wednesday night Explorers' meeting.

Wheel of Fire members-only services were stripped down and hardcore, compared to services open to the public. There were fewer attendees—no Outer Wheel at all—so Kori joined Flicker Midwheel, feeling like an impostor. Promus and the Inner Wheel members wore just their jeans and orange T-shorts. No capes, no incense, no healings. Apparently Promus didn't feel the need to show off to his own people.

"My sons and daughters, the Apocalypse is coming soon, sooner than you think," he preached. "Michael has revealed to me the exact day, down to the minute."

Murmurs arose from the congregation.

"When?"

"So soon?"

"Are we ready?"

Promos raised his palms to silence them. "I won't disclose the exact time to you yet because you must not fear it. Your job is to live in the present. Every day you must struggle because the Church of Wheel of Fire has enemies. Who are our enemies? All those on earth who do not believe my true word. You must be on your guard, ever vigilant. Satan is able to appear to you in many forms: a horse, a beautiful woman, a friend. You must be willing to kill him, even if he happens to appear as your own birth mother. You must kill him or be killed. Yes, my sons and daughters, there is no more glorious death than that of a martyr for our faith, for me your Real Father, for Michael the Archangel, for God."

"Yes, Real Father," the Wheelers replied hypnotically.

Following the sermon was the prayer to Michael the Archangel, and then the chant. As Kori clasped hands with Flicker, she realized she had been looking forward to this part of the service. When Flicker squeezed her hand, Kori passed the pulse on with a tiny thrill, which increased in intensity each round.

"Come, spirit of Michael," said Promus.

"Come, spirit of Michael," responded the congregation.

Around and around the Wheel streaked the pulse, faster and faster. Over an hour passed. Kori scalp prickled with heat, and her hands were slick with sweat. Some believers spoke in tongues, and flames appeared over nearly everyone's head. Kori stared at the spot of fire over Flicker, wondering how it was produced.

"Look away!" she urged in a hushed tone. "The spirit of Michael is strong enough to blind you." The overhead lights switched on. "Did the spirit come to you, Kori?" asked Flicker, flushed with euphoria.

"No," she said flatly.

Flicker clutched Kori's shoulders and looked fervently into her eyes. "Oh, the spirit *will* come, and when it does, it's the greatest feeling ever. Are you sure you didn't feel *something*? Just a tinge?"

Kori thought of the little jolts of excitement the pulses delivered, but replied, "I *feel* hungry! Let's eat!"

She peered into the dining hall and found it dark. No yummy feast was waiting. A solemn, middle-aged woman, wearing oversized dark glasses, glided up to them.

"Hi, Mona," Flicker greeted her. The woman held out a small ivory envelope. "What's this?" Flicker asked. Mona shrugged and ambled away, as Flicker tore open the envelope and removed a plain notecard. "Oh, wow!" she gasped. "This is amazing! This has never happened to me. It's an invitation to dine with Inner Wheel!"

"Oh! Congratulations," said Kori, "I'll leave you to it."

"Wait, you're invited, too!" Flicker grabbed her hand, but she balked.

"Are you sure? I'm not even a member!"

Flicker held up the card. "It says 'You and your guest are cordially invited.' Gee, I wonder if Promus will be there!"

Still Kori hesitated. "I should go. It's a school night. My mother expects me home early."

"And miss this opportunity? Come on! Don't be shy." Flicker encircled Kori's wrist and led her down a darkened corridor and into a cramped, empty room with a low ceiling, barely large enough for six chairs and a circular table, dimly lit by a dish of fire.

"Oh, they're not here yet," said Flicker. They sat silently, for several minutes, Flicker shifting nervously in her seat, staring at the door.

"Are you sure we're in the right place?" Kori asked.

"Shh!"

At last Ashe, Flame, and Stix entered the room, carrying food. On Flame's tray were six eggs and glasses of milk, cream rising to their frothy tops. She sat at the table, cracked an egg into each glass and stirred. Stix set before each of them small bowls of raw almonds, and Ashe's offering was plates of chopped persimmons.

Flame set a glass before Kori. "Here, drink. Fresh from the goat."

Imagining bacteria swimming in the raw milk and salmonella infesting the egg, Kori drew back. "So you do eat raw food. You told me you didn't."

Flame's sneer twisted into a smile. "If we had served you raw food the first night you were here, would you have returned? We have to reveal our ways gradually to our recruits; otherwise, we'd scare them off."

Everyone at the table laughed, everyone but Kori.

Flicker took a long pull of the warm goat's milk and raw egg concoction. "Try it, Kori. It's packed with protein."

"No, thanks."

Ashe reached across the table and tapped his finger next to her glass. "Drink," he demanded in a steely, even voice.

Kori took a small sip.

"Now, Kori Lawton, tell us your intentions," Ashe ordered.

"My intentions?"

"Are you joining us?" Flame asked pointedly.

"Um…no."

"Then why are you here?" Flame pressed her.

"Flicker invited me. I just wanted to know more about Wheel of Fire."

"Are you writing a report for your little Explorer class?" Ashe asked sarcastically. "This is a recruitment service."

"Oh, I didn't know," Kori said in a small voice. She looked over at Flicker, whose eyes were downcast.

Stix pushed his heavy, horned-rimmed glasses up his nose to peer into Kori's face. "Certainly you've felt the power of St Michael, by now," he said gently. "What's stopping you from going with the flow of the spirit?"

Kori's heart pounded. Her mind whirled with visions of escape, sprinting down the dark gravel road, jumping into her truck, and speeding away forever, and yet her limbs were frozen in place.

"You're on the fence, Kori Lawton," said Ashe, "and there are no fences at Armageddon. Fences are made of wood and wood *burns* like the black souls of sinners."

"*Have* you received the spirit of Michael?" asked Flame.

Her throat was thick with her one sip of goat's milk. Kori gulped and said, "No."

"Hmm…three sessions here and no Michael." Ashe shook his head. "That's tragic, real tragic. Maybe you're not meant to be saved. Not all of Satan's minions are serial killers and child molesters, you know. Thousands of people who fall into Satan's ranks are just like you."

"Millions," interjected Flame.

"Billions," said Ashe. "Seemingly good, innocent people who never got around to accepting Jesus Christ as their savior and Promus as their general. And what happens to people just like you, Kori Lawton? Eternal damnation." Ashe leered and fluttered his fingers in her face. "Good-bye, Kori. Welcome to the fiery abyss."

"No, Kori, no! Don't go to Satan!" Flicker pounced, wrapping her bony arms around her waist.

"Damn it, Flicker, stay out of this," said Ashe. "It's up to Kori to decide her own fate."

Flicker let her arms flop to her sides.

Stix gave Kori's hand a reassuring pat. "You don't want to belong to Satan, now do you?"

"No," she said.

"Fine," said Flame. "That's a start. Now, we've been very generous to you, welcoming you into our home, sharing our feasts. It's time you gave back." She extended her hand.

From her first visit, Kori had learned not to carry a purse into Promisedland. She had only her keys, driver's license, and a few small bills stuffed into her pants pocket. She gave Flame all the money she had on her.

She counted it disdainfully. "Seven bucks? That's all we're worth to you? How about you hand over the pink slip to your truck?"

"How do you know I have a truck?" Kori asked.

"We know everything we need to know about you," said Ashe. "Who do you think you're dealing with?"

"I need my truck. It's my transportation."

"Okay, then. Let's use it as transportation," said Flame. "Let's drive into town and clean out your fat bank account."

"My dad gave me that money for college!"

Ashe shook his head. "You seem like a smart girl, Kori Lawton. Doesn't she seem like a smart girl to you, Flame?"

She flipped her long, red hair back over her shoulders. "She seemed smart at first, but she sure is slow to catch on."

"You don't need college now," Stix explained, enunciating as if he were speaking to a first-grader. "Promus will teach you everything you need to know."

"I want to get a degree in criminology and fight crime."

"You can do all that in just a couple years?" asked Ashe. "That's about all the time you've got left on this earth."

"If that," said Flame. "I doubt if it's half that."

"It would be folly if you spent your last days on earth preparing for the wrong thing," said Stix. "It's not crime you need to fight, Kori. It's Satan."

She felt panicky, Promus's threatening sermons echoing in her head. What if she really *was* on her way to hell?

"Write us a check. Right now," said Flame. "Say, for a couple a hundred. No, make it a thousand."

"I don't have a checkbook," Kori said meekly.

"You're wasting our time. Flicker, show your guest out." Flame pointed to the door where Promus suddenly appeared.

"Hey! Hey! What's going on? This is no way to treat our guest!" He stepped into the room and flicked on the overhead light, causing the others to squint in the sudden brightness. He sauntered toward the group, his thumbs hooked casually in his jean pockets. He stood behind Flicker and began massaging her shoulders as he stared intently into Kori's face. Flicker seemed to melt into his hands, rolling her eyes in a near swoon. "We're interested in *you*, Kori Lawton, not your money."

"Easy for you to say, Vince" said Flame, "seeing how you're so much better at spending it than raising it."

"Watch your tone, Sharon." His hands slid up Flicker's throat and his thumbs pressed into the base of her skull. "I've prayed to Michael about this. He told me that Kori Lawton will be of great service to us."

"Of great service?" Flame mocked. "Oh, yeah, Vince, I'll bet."

Promus's hands dropped to his sides, causing Flicker's neck to jerk backward. Promus/Vince and Flame/Sharon were locked in an intense staring match.

"Service, yes!" exclaimed Stix.

"She can be a gatherer," Flicker suggested cheerfully. "Ember can always use more help."

"She can fund raise," said Ashe.

Kori held up both palms. "Really, I'm not interested in—"

"You'll do both," Flame ordered gruffly.

"You'll have to do those jobs well, Kori," said Stix, "to prove that you are worthy of us."

Kori shook her head vigorously. "This is a mistake. I have to go."

"She'll do fine," said Promus, gazing into Kori's eyes like a kindly minister. He placed his broad, overly warm hand on her cheek, and it took all her will not to recoil from his touch. "I have plans for you, Kori Lawton. You may well become a member of my special task force."

Flame slammed her palm on the table. "You don't need a special task force anymore, Vince. You agreed to that after your last little escapade."

"Easy, Flame." Ashe placed his hand on hers to calm her, but she flicked it away.

"Dear Flame, you seem conflicted," Promus said, a mocking sweetness invading his tone. "Weren't you just complaining about the state of our finances?"

"We can sell off some property if we need more ready cash," said Flame.

"I *like* my property," said Promus. He plucked an almond out of the bowl, tossed it in the air, and caught it in his mouth. Chewing, he grinned. "And special task force is so much fun."

Flame leaned toward him and muttered through clenched teeth, "You know it's too risky to—" Approaching footsteps interrupted her.

Ember entered the room, and without a word, began collecting the dirty dishes. Kori thought she was purposely ignoring her, but then, just before she turned to leave, she flashed Kori a piercing look, eyes wide, brows crushed together. It startled Kori and yet she didn't know what it meant. Was Ember merely surprised to see her at an Inner Wheel meeting or was she warning her away?

Kori couldn't get out of Promisedland fast enough.

She arose the next morning and peered into her dresser mirror. Pointing to her face, splotched red with acne, she said, "You're not going back! Not ever, got that? Too bad for Flicker and Mrs. Jamison stuck there. You can't save everybody." Then she fell into bed and pulled the covers over her head.

A short while later, her mom came in to see why she wasn't up, getting ready for school.

"I'm not going. I don't feel well," Kori told her.

Cindy pressed the back of her fingers against Kori's cheek, where Promus's hand had lay. "You do feel a bit warm. I'll call in your absence."

Kori dozed. The signal of an incoming text woke her around nine. She checked her phone.

"Where are you?" Luke had written.

"Home."

"Cold? Flu?"

"I don't feel like going to schoolitis."

He responded with "LOL. Miss U."

Her stomach growled. She remembered she hadn't eaten dinner, and a bagel and cream cheese sounded wonderful. She was surprised to find her mom in jeans and a sweatshirt, seated at the kitchen table, lingering over her coffee and the morning paper.

"You didn't go into work?" Kori asked.

"I wanted to be here in case you need anything."

"Gee, thanks, but I'm fine, really." Kori toasted her bagel, warmed a mug of coffee, and sat with her mom. It was nice, just the two them, without Vaughn lurking. "Hey, Mom, I've got a question. When Dad left me his truck, did he really give-give it to me, like he changed the name on the pink slip, or did he like just say it's mine?"

"What difference does it make? You're driving it."

"I know, but I just realized the other day I don't really know if it's legally mine."

Cindy peered over her newspaper at Kori. "There was really no point in changing the pink slip. For one thing, your car insurance is cheaper. But if it really bothers you, I suppose you could contact your dad and––"

"No, no. It's fine the way it is. I was just wondering is all." Several minutes passed, and then Kori asked, "Mom? Can I just *see* the pink slip?"

Cindy twisted in her chair and pointed to a drawer where the family kept receipts and other papers. Kori found the certificate of title for the truck, and it did have her dad's name on it: Donald J. Lawton. She couldn't legally sign the truck over to the Wheel even if Flame or Ashe managed to hypnotize her or drug her or trick her in some way. Even though she had no intentions of returning to Promisedland, that Inner Wheel meeting had shaken her.

"Okay?" Cindy asked.

Kori nodded, returning to her place at the table. "It's good to know legal stuff, you know." She clutched her mug, deep in thought. Then she noticed her mom was talking, and she didn't know what she was saying. Cindy paused, apparently waiting for her response. "What's that?"

"You haven't been listening to me. If fact, you've been distracted quite a lot lately. What's going on with you?"

"Nothing. Everything's fine."

"You break out when things aren't fine. Are you still upset about that missed call from you dad?"

"Kinda, sorta. Do you think it was about his coming home for Christmas?"

"I wouldn't know."

"Do you think it's about him *not* coming home? Why doesn't he communicate with us more?"

"Partly because he's not in a position to and partly because—well, communication has never been one of his strong points."

Kori rubbed the bumpy pimples on her forehead. "Um…Mom? Later on, could we go down to the bank? I want you to cosign on my savings account."

"That's your money! What have I got to do with it?"

"You're my mom. It would be good to have another name on it in case of…in case of an emergency or something."

"Your dad has dumped a whole lot of dough in that account since he's been in the military. I don't want him accusing me of trying to get my hands on it."

"But what if I'm tempted to blow it on something stupid?"

Cindy chuckled. "Like what? We didn't nickname you 'Squirrel' for nothing." As a kid, Kori squirreled away any money that she got, mostly for her birthday and Christmas.

"Uh, well…Luke and I went into Bakersfield the other day, and I saw this awesome snowboarding package," Kori lied. "It was like a thousand bucks, and I was totally tempted to go for it."

Cindy folded her newspaper and leaned toward Kori. "Is Luke pressuring you to loan him money?"

"This has nothing to do with Luke."

"Have you developed a drug habit?"

"Real funny, Mom!"

"Well, I don't know. Imagine how surprised I was when I discovered Jared was using meth *and* had joined a gang."

"I'm not Jared."

"Of course not, sweetie. Speaking of your brother…"

"Thanksgiving is coming up." Kori hated visiting Jared in prison, especially on holidays. "Don't let Vaughn come."

Cindy sighed, resting her chin in her hand. "What's so bad about Vaughn?"

"He's a douchebag."

Cindy hooted to the ceiling. It was not the reaction Kori expected.

"Why don't you just get a divorce and date someone who's good enough for you?"

"Maybe I don't want a divorce." Cindy raised her eyebrows with a confiding smirk. "Vaughn's more into me than I'm into him. He treats me like a princess."

"But you're cheating on Dad!"

Cindy began to jiggle the leg crossed over her knee. "He started it."

Kori sucked in breath. "Since when?"

"Since you were…. Nope, I take pride in not dumping on your dad to you, even though it's tempting. I've already said too much."

"Okay, then. Why do you and Vaughn sneak around?"

"Honest to God, Kori. You've lived in Goldhurst your whole life, and you still don't know how a small town works."

"People talk. I get it." Kori took a huge bite of her bagel, causing Cindy to grin.

"Feeling better?"

Kori nodded, chewing. "Yeah. I guess I was just tired."

"Nothing wrong with taking an occasional rest day. Explorers ran pretty late. Or did you hang out with Luke afterward?"

"No, but what if I did? I thought you liked him."

"He seems like a nice boy. I just hope you don't get too serious. Take it from one who knows from experience: you don't know enough about yourself in high school to pick a husband."

"*Husband*?" Kori shrieked. "Yikes! Luke is a *junior*! I'm going away to college next year."

Cindy pointed a finger at her. "Just see that you do."

Kori was glad she had stayed home from school that day. She and her mom had cleared the air between them, and Cindy finally did agree to cosign on her bank account. Walking out of the bank that afternoon with the sun streaking through the golden leaves, Kori felt so relieved that she was almost giddy.

If Ashe was right about her going to hell, at least she was going to college first.

Chapter Nine

Kori was in her robe, settled on the sofa with her second mug of coffee. It was a lazy Sunday morning. Her mom was in town buying groceries, and she was home alone, daydreaming about the Harvest Dance, the previous evening. How lovely it had been, swaying in Luke's arms beneath a revolving disco ball rather than chanting and squeezing people's sweaty hands in a crazy Wheel service.

Kori heard the gravel crunch as a vehicle pulled into the driveway. She peeked through the blinds and was shocked to see an orange Wheel of Fire van idling out in front of her house. She had never given the Wheel her address! She had deleted their contact information from her phone and blocked the number Flicker had used to reach her. What could they possibly want from her now?

She tiptoed to the front door and spied out the peephole. Ashe was in the driver's seat, Flame was riding shotgun, and at least a dozen Wheelers were on board. Flicker jumped out of the vehicle, leaped up the porch steps, and rang the bell. Kori peered out at her pale face and skinny body lost in baggy, worn men's clothes. She felt a rush of affection. Poor, sweet Flicker, lost to the world.

Kori opened the door a crack.

"Oh, hi, come on," Flicker said, as if picking her up had been prearranged.

"What?"

She pressed her hand to her waist impatiently. "You forgot? You promised Flame you'd help us fund raise."

"No, I didn't."

"Yes, you did. I heard you."

Kori sighed. It was pointless to argue. "Well, I'm not interested."

"Get dressed. We'll wait for you." Flicker hopped off the porch.

"Didn't you hear me? I'm not coming!" Kori called after her.

Flicker turned, looked Kori in the eye, and replied pointedly, "We'll wait for you."

How did Flicker know that the last thing Kori wanted was her mom to return home to find an orange Wheel of Fire van parked in their drive? What choice did she have? In minutes, she was seated in the van—no purse, phone, or keys—heading up Highway 99 toward Fresno, without telling her mom or anybody where she was going.

As rain began to splatter the windows, the Wheelers broke out in "Onward, Christian Soldiers." Everyone joined in but Scorch, pressed against the door with closed eyes. Kori was uneasy about being around the creepy guy who had tried to rough up Luke, but all the others seemed nice.

Spark, who was a Kindergarten teacher, led the group in a rousing "Wheels on the Bus" with accompanying hand motions. It was all so silly, Kori had to laugh. After the singing she got into a conversation with Spark who explained that everyone who had paying jobs outside of Promisedland signed their paychecks over to Promus.

"But don't you ever want your own money?" Kori asked.

"What for?" asked Blaze. "Real Father gives us everything we could ever want, and—"

"He paid for my college. I wouldn't even be a teacher if it weren't for him," said Spark. She held up the plain, gold wedding band on her finger. "We wouldn't be married."

Blaze hugged her and kissed her on the cheek.

Over an hour later, Ashe pulled into the crowded River Park Shopping Censer. Flame divided the fundraisers into three teams of "Four Horsemen." Kori and Flicker were grouped with Glow and Scorch.

"Now stick with your assigned Horsemen," ordered Ashe. He and Flame apparently were going to wait in the van with the heater blasting away.

As the automatic side door slid opened, Scorch hesitated, gazing out at the rain pelting down. "I don't know, man. It's pretty ugly out there."

Ashe reached around the car seat and gave him a shove. “Go on, move it! When you’ve each got two hundred dollars to show for yourself, we’ll let you back in the van.”

“Come on, guys!” exclaimed Spark. “Let’s score for Real Father!”

The Wheelers cheered as they leaped from the van. Flicker bounded enthusiastically across the parking lot so that Kori had to jog to keep up with her. How could she bring herself to beg money for Wheel of Fire? She hoped she wouldn’t run into anybody she knew.

“Hey, hold up,” said Scorch in a grumpy tone. Glow shuffled far behind him.

Kori and Flicker waited for them under an awning outside California Pizza Kitchen, which looked warm and inviting inside and smelled delicious.

“What did Glow do to earn her fire name?” Kori asked Flicker.

“She gave Promus the car she was living in.”

“Where is it now?”

“I don’t know. I guess Flame sold it. She’s the money person, in case you haven’t figured that out.”

“What’s Scorch’s story?” Kori asked. “He looks like a meth head.”

“He’s local. He and his pal Match are both from Goldhurst.”

“Match?” Kori looked around at the other Wheel members. “Which one is he?”

“He’s not here. Flame tries to keep those two apart.” She leaned into Kori and whispered, “Real Father had to bail them out of jail once.”

“What for?”

“Don’t know, but they’re both Inner Wheel.”

Kori reared her head back. “*Why*?”

“Exactly.” Flicker mouth tensed. “I’d like to know why them and not me. I’ve done everything I can to please Real Father, but…” She grabbed Kori’s arm and jumped on the balls of her feet. “I’m so glad you’re here! Let’s be the first ones to make quota!”

The method of fund raising seemed to be up to the individual Wheelers. Some of them handed matchbooks to people, and then asked for donations. Others bought boxes of candy or small candles at a discount store for a dollar and sold them for five. Some merely panhandled. Out of her backpack, Flicker removed tin cans with photos of emaciated children of Bangladesh taped on them and passed them around.

"This money isn't going to starving children!" Kori said.

"So what?" Scorch grinned, revealing his rotten, jagged teeth. "We need it more than a bunch of potbellied brats."

Kori looked down at the suffering children on her can. "That's just wrong."

"Oh, please!" Glow rolled her bloodshot eyes. "Let's just get this over with."

People were streaming in and out of the restaurant, and for the first hour, the four of them did a pretty good business in spare change and dollars bills. They drifted farther and father apart until Kori noticed Flicker was the only one around. "Where's Scorch and Glow?"

Flicker shrugged. "Probably Scorch slipped off to have a cigarette, and Glow went for a beer. They're both useless. I don't know why Promus keeps them around."

"Can't anyone who wants to be in Wheel of Fire live at Promisedland?"

"It's not a homeless shelter. Residents have to pull their weight."

"You really think an angel appears to Promus?" Kori blurted.

Flicker tilted her head, her face bearing its lighted expression. "Why do you struggle against the faith, Kori?"

"Have other people seen him talking to the angel?"

"Yes! Sometimes Flame, Ashe, and Stix go into the backcountry with him. Promus rides his black stallion, Flame has a gold palomino, Ashe is on a chestnut sorrel, and Stix rides a gray Andalusian, you know, like the Four Horsemen of the Apocalypse."

Kori creased her brow. "No, tell me."

"It's in the Bible. Read Revelations. It's not like Promus is making this stuff up."

"So Michael the Archangel appears to *four* people?"

"Just Promus. But the others know the angel is there because they see and hear Promus talking to him."

Kori rolled her eyes.

Flicker counted her money. "Sixteen thirty-seven," she announced. "What about you?"

"Thirteen something." Just then a man dropped a five into Kori's can. "Eighteen! I capped you!"

"Oh, yeah? We'll see about that!" Flicker began belting out, "'Anything you can do, I can do better. I can do anything better than you!'" She really did have a great singing voice. Shoppers gathered to listen to her. Kori remembered a silly line dance from P.E. and sashayed around the perimeter of the crowd collecting money. Their routine was a big success until a waiter came out of the restaurant and shooed them off.

Laughing, they dashed down a walkway, splashing through standing water, until they stopped breathlessly at a bench in a sheltered alcove.

"What was that song you were singing?" Kori asked.

"It's from *Annie Get Your Gun.* I had the lead in my high school musical." She smiled ruefully. "Back in the day, I wanted to sing on Broadway."

"What happened to that?"

Flicker looked away, the color drained from her face. Then she smiled brightly, fingering Kori's sleeve. "Oh, I wish you'd join the Wheel! I haven't had a real friend in so long!"

"I don't think Promus wants you to have a friend. I think he wants to keep you all to himself."

Flicker scowled. "Sometimes I think he doesn't even know I exist."

"I saw the way he massaged your back. He's really fond of you."

"You think? He hadn't touched me in months. The best day of my life was the day I joined the Wheel. He told me that he knew Satan was tempting me into a terrible sin. He sat me on his lap and rocked me like a baby. I cried and cried and he stroked my hair."

"What sin?"

Flicker dropped her chin. "Have sex with a married man," she whispered shamefully.

"Were you living with your parents then?"

"No, no. I…ran away."

Kori struggled to control her excitement. She knew she had to choose her questions carefully to keep Flicker talking. "You lived on the *street*?"

"No, I was a live-in nanny. I took a bus to Sacramento, looked on craigslist, and got the job. They had two sweet kids, Logan and Jaden."

"Were the parents Wheelers?"

"Oh, no. They didn't go to church. I'd been raised in a Christian home and missed it. Barry—the dad—was hitting on me. We had a couple heavy make out sessions and I was feeling guilty. I knew I had to get back to Jesus. The Wheel came into town every other week and held services in a vacant store in the neighborhood, and I started attending. I was drawn to Promus from the start. The day I joined, he summoned me during the service. He told everyone to pray for me because Satan was trying to own me. I had agreed to meet Barry at a motel that afternoon. After the service was when Promus sat me on his lap and prayed with me. He told me I shouldn't return to the Snells, not even to get my things. It hurt me to desert those kids. It hurt to leave the pearl necklace my mom had given me, but I got into the Wheel van bound for Promisedland and never looked back."

Kori felt so close to knowing Flicker's true identity that her arms tingled with anticipation. "Where do your parents live?"

Flicker stared across the rainy parking lot, a far-off look of reminiscing on her face. Abruptly, she snapped out of it. She dumped the contents of her can into her backpack and jumped to her feet. Water oozed out of her thin, worn canvas shoes, and she laughed. "Let's get going."

"What about your parents? Don't you feel bad that they don't know where you are?"

"Oh, they know."

"*They do*?"

"Uh-huh. I called them from the Snells to tell them I was okay. They hired a P.I. who found me in Promisedland last year."

"And?"

Flicker shrugged. "They tried to get me to defect so I had to take a Shunning Vow." Her head snapped, as she searched frantically in all directions. "Where is everybody? Let's go out there and hit people up as they get out of their cars."

"We'll get drenched."

"The more pathetic we look, the more we'll score."

Kori watched Flicker lope toward the parking lot, but she didn't budge. All the hours she had wasted searching through the Missing Persons files, hoping to inform Flicker's parents about her whereabouts, when they had known all along! Shunning Vow—hell! Only Satan himself could think of such a cruel way to tear families apart.

Flicker whirled around, grinning. "Come on, Kori. We've got work to do."

She shouted back, "This is no way to live."

Flicker flapped her arms in a silly dance, water dripping off her nose. "It's the only way!"

"Having a good job, a warm house, a loving family. That's a life."

Flicker's smile faded slightly. "I have those things."

"Begging is not a job. I'm done. I'm calling my boyfriend to come get me!"

Flicker dashed up to her. "Oh, Kori, don't! Please, don't! Ashe will blame me. He'll punish me for breaking the Rule of the Four Horsemen. Oh, me and my big mouth!" Flicker grasped Kori's sleeve with icy fingers. "Wait for me in that coffee shop. I'll raise both our quotas and come get you."

"I could use a steaming mocha right now."

"Don't spend any of Real Father's money. That's sacrilege."

"He can spare the change," Kori shot back.

Cupping her warm drink, she watched Flicker through the window, working the lot. Parking places were scarce, and when a car backed out of one, Flicker stood in the empty space and waved another car in, as if she held some authority. When the shoppers got out of their cars, she hit them up for a tip.

The rain dwindled to a drizzle. Two guys emerged from a black SUV and stood talking to Flicker. One was short and muscular with a full black beard, and the taller one was paunchy. The men slowly moved around Flicker, so that she was wedged between them and their vehicle. The bearded man took a step toward Flicker, crowding her in a menacing way and gesturing toward his car.

Kori bolted from the shop and sprinted toward Flicker, shouting her name.

"Kori!" Flicker called back.

The pot-bellied man scowled and nudged his companion toward their vehicle. They drove off in a hurry.

"Those guys gave me a twenty," Flicker said, "but I really had to earn it."

"What do you mean?"

"Oh, they thought they knew a lot about the Wheel. The short one called it a cult and said Promus was a con man. The fat one goes, 'Here, let us take you to a better life.' He started pushing me toward their car."

"Scary! Have you ever seen them before?"

Flicker gave a terse shake of her head, her lips pressed firmly together.

Kori and Flicker began working the parking lot together, Scorch and Glow nowhere in sight. It was after eight, nearly all the stores closed and the crowd thinned out, when they finally raised their combined four hundred dollars. Ashe and Flame welcomed them into the warm van and handed them ginger root scraped into hot water for tea and dried fruit and nuts for a meal. It took a couple more hours for the rest of the Wheelers to return to the van, everybody except Scorch and Glow. Flame counted out the haul, nearly two thousand dollars. Scorch climbed in the van and handed Flame a small wad of bills, mostly ones. She scowled, but she didn't say anything. Finally Glow shuffled up to the van, a bit tipsy. The automatic door didn't open for her.

"Ah, let me in, Ashe."

"Let's see what you've got first." He reached out the driver's window and took Glow's collecting can and dumped its contents into Flame's lap.

"Twenty-two, twenty-seven," she announced.

"Looks like you've come up short, Glow," Ashe said out the window. "Again."

"I'll do better next time." Glow placed her trembling hand on the van door. "Open up."

Ashe put the van into reverse and drove away. "Glow needs a new name," he said. "Burn."

"Burn who?" asked Flame.

"Burn Out." he replied.

They burst out laughing, and some of the other Wheelers joined in.

Kori gazed out the back window at Glow, deserted and alone, swaying forlornly in the dark and rain.

It was after eleven when Kori finally reached home. Her mom dashed out onto the porch to greet her as she leaped out of the Wheel of Fire van.

"Kori! What is going on? I've been frantic! I had no idea where you were, and—Jesus—is that cult trying to *recruit* you?"

"Let's go inside, Mom. I'll tell you everything."

Seated at the kitchen table, scarfing down her mom's delicious ham and scalloped potatoes, Kori told her the whole story, how she had first seen Flicker and wanted to rescue her. She confessed to attending several Wheel services as a way of getting closer to her, but she stopped short of mentioning Luke's mom.

"You're not making sense, Kori. Why would you go to so much trouble for someone you don't even know?"

"I have gotten to know her, Mom. We're friends. She's living in misery. You should see how badly they treat her."

"But you don't have any interest in joining yourself?"

"No, Mom!" Greedily, Kori scraped her fork against her empty plate. She'd never been so hungry and grateful for her mom's cooking. "Is there more?"

Cindy served her a second helping and watched her eat. "Now I remember you wanting me to attend a Wheel of Fire service with you. I wish I had. You've always had a spiritual bent, Squirrel. Remember when you were in the fourth grade, and you made all of us go to a different church each Sunday, hoping we'd find just the right one?"

Kori nodded, her mouth full.

"Wheel of Fire's brand of faith is quite persuasive. I'm afraid they'll suck you in." Cindy gasped, her hand flying to her throat. "This is why you insisted I cosign on your bank account!"

Kori winced. "They already asked for it. My truck, too. But honest, Mom, I was only going to their services to visit Flicker."

"Promise me you'll never go back!"

Kori raised her palm like she was taking an oath. "No worries, Mom. I learned my lesson today. I'm done." It crossed her mind that she had already learned her lesson, at the Inner Wheel meeting. She pressed her napkin to her mouth and belched quietly. "Excuse me. Is there dessert?"

"Apple and pomegranate pie!" Cindy jumped to her feet and kissed the top of Kori's head.

Chapter Ten

The house was filled with delicious turkey smells, but Kori couldn't relax and enjoy Thanksgiving, not until she and her mom visited Jared in Corcoran Prison. He'd served a little over a year of his seven-year sentence, and they didn't visit him often. Holidays were the worst, so sad to see Jared stuck in the pen, instead of home with the family.

Cindy scurried into the kitchen, patting her hair in place. "Do I look okay?" She had reached into the back of her closet and come up with an old pantsuit with baggy dress trousers. She liked wearing form-fitting stretchy pants, but she was hypersensitive about the prison's visitors' dress code.

"Fine, Mom. Just don't cry," said Kori.

"I won't." Cindy thrashed her lashes and turned her face from Kori. "Let me check the turkey, and we'll be on our way." She opened the oven and pulled out the rack to baste the turkey. "This is silly, a whole big bird for the two of us. Too bad the prison won't allow outside food."

"I love leftovers," Kori said, forcing cheerfulness into her tone. At least Vaughn wouldn't be around today. He had invited Cindy and Kori to his mother's house in Porterville, but Kori had said she'd rather eat McDonald's than pretend to be part of Vaughn's extended family. "Maybe Wheel of Fire will have you," Cindy had retorted sarcastically, which had stung Kori. She had had no contact with the Wheel for over two weeks, but Flicker and Luke's mom were often on her mind.

Kori and Cindy didn't have much to say to each other on the short drive up Highway 43. Cindy leaned over the steering wheel, peering out the windshield, tears streaming silently down her face. Anyone who called Jared a mama's boy would have hell to pay, but that's what he was. When

Cindy had returned home from the hospital with newborn Kori, Jared had dashed outside to greet her, ecstatically shouting, "Mommy! Mommy!" He took one look at the infant in her arms and asked, "Who is *his* Mommy?"

Jared had a way of presenting a false image of himself to his family and hiding what he was really up to, smiling like the Cheshire cat. The night he was arrested was the first the family had heard that he was a Ghoul gang member. All the way down to the police station, Bud Lawton had ranted how worthless their son was, but Cindy defended him. "The school never let him play sports," she said. "All he ever wanted was to be accepted, be a part of a team." Bud groaned. "The Goldhurst Ghouls! Some team. He could have played school sports if he cared enough to keep his grades up. And how many times has he been suspended for acting up?"

Kori had kept quiet in the backseat, listening to her parents argue. Jared had never *felt* he was good enough for anything. He had been small for his age, with hair so blond it was almost white. Bigger boys taunted him, calling him "girly," "wuss," "homo," and he would fly at them in a rage, knowing he'd get his ass kicked. In high school he lifted weights, built and raced faster and faster cars, but it took the Ghouls to make him feel like a man.

In her future as a detective, Kori would have to get used to going into prisons, but right now they gave her the creeps. Arriving at Corcoran, she and her mom waited to go through security, and then they waited to be led into a visiting room, which was already crowded and noisy with inmates and their visitors talking loudly, little kids yelling, and babies crying. The room was arranged with chairs clustered around small tables, and the prisoners had to sit facing the surveillance cameras. A correctional officer was sent to release Jared from his cell. Kori waited nervously while her mom fidgeted with her rings, sliding them on and off.

Finally, Jared appeared. Unlike most of the other convicts, he was clean cut, with no visible tats. Kori was especially relieved not to see the traditional purple teardrop beneath his eye that indicated he'd been in prison.

Cindy threw her arms around her son, her shoulders heaving. She covered her eyes with the back of her hand and rushed out of the room.

"Ah, shit." Jared threw himself in a chair and patted his pocket for cigarettes. He didn't have any; there was no smoking in the visitors' room. "Can you stop her from coming? I hate the damn crying."

"She tries not to," said Kori. "How's it going?"

"It's going. It's prison." He smiled at her. Jared wasn't one to express affection, but Kori saw it in his eyes. It felt good just to *see* him, to know he was still breathing. "You still playing cops and robbers, 'lil sis?"

"Dude, check this out!" Kori sat in profile and flexed her bicep.

He laughed. "There's mosquitos this time of year?"

"These are my guns! I'm getting strong, Jared, I could pick you up!"

"Don't." He raised both palms, laughing.

"I've got a workout buddy. I think you might know him—Luke Jamison. Actually, he's kind of a boyfriend."

"No lie? I never pictured you with a grease monkey."

Somehow that hurt. "He's a smart dude. He's cool to hang out with."

"Okay, fine. Didn't mean to dis him."

"Are you staying out of trouble, Jared, really? What do the Ghouls expect of you in here?"

"Not a fucking thing. We have each other's backs, that's it."

That could keep Jared out of a fight or force him into one. Kori hated to admit a gang affiliation would help him stay alive in prison, but she knew it was true.

"Are you still working on-line for your auto tech certificate?" she asked.

"Yup. Got a job inside, too. Machine maintenance. Could reduce my sentence."

Kori nodded her approval. There was hope for him yet. He was only twenty-two. Maybe he'd plea bargain yet or win his appeal. "Dad's got leave the middle of next month," she said. "He'll probably be with us the next time we visit."

Jared's eyes flashed with anger. "Did he say he was coming home?"

"Where else would he go on leave?"

"Kori." He pronounced her name slowly. "Did he give specific information, his flight number, what time to pick him up at the airport?"

"Not yet, but—"

"I hate to be the one to disappoint daddy's little girl, but I'm just trying to let you down easy. He's moved on. He'd got another woman."

A ripple of pain coursed though her body. She was sorry she had even mentioned their dad. She knew Jared wasn't as eager to see him as she was. "Who told you that?"

He tapped his temple. "Men know these things about other men."

Kori didn't argue. She was looking forward to proving him wrong.

Cindy reappeared, all put together, her makeup fixed, bearing an armload of gifts from the vending machines. Jared told her what he had told Kori about his job and the on-line program, just the good news, Jared style.

"Did your sister tell you she's thinking about joining Wheel of Fire?" Cindy sucked her lower lip.

"Mom!" Kori looked at Jared. "Not true. I just met a girl in there, and we got kinda friendly."

"She's been attending their services," said Cindy. "She even drove up to Fresno with them to fund raise."

"Mom!" Kori pleaded again. "I explained all that." She told Jared, "I was just trying to get closer to Flick—my friend. Find out her real name, where her parents live. The Wheel doesn't let their members talk about their past."

"I know it." Jared held his steady gaze on Kori so long it made her want to squirm. "They call it a church, but it's a cult, a destructive cult. Their leader—that Promus dude? He's insane."

Kori flashed on Promus swinging a rifle by its trigger guard, his black eyes boring into her. "How would you know?"

"Two guys I know got sucked in."

"Who?"

"Travis Collins and Joe Mattingly. You run into them?"

Kori shook her head.

"They were Ghouls, but gangbanging was too tame for them. You think they joined Wheel of Fire to *pray*?" Jared shook his head. "Keep the fuck away, Kori."

"I will!" she nearly shouted. She glared at her mom, who gazed innocently back.

Chapter Eleven

Kori cut across the municipal park and spotted Flicker at In-N-Out, up to her old tricks. She was seated on a cement bench, a cardboard tray of french fries before her, glancing around and chewing furtively like a rodent.

A rush of affection flooded Kori's heart. She had to at least go over and say hi.

"Hey, Kori! We miss you," Flicker said, around a mouthful of french fries. "*I* miss you."

"What brings you to town?"

Flicker nodded toward Comstock Market. "Ember and her gathering committee are doing the grocery shopping. She gave me a little money to come over here." Flicker smiled sheepishly. "She's sweet like that."

Kori glanced over her friend's chapped lips, cracked and bitten nails, and frayed cuffs. "How are you?"

"Oh, great! My favorite Wheel holiday is coming up. The Winter Solstice Celebration."

"Isn't that a pagan tradition?"

Flicker shrugged. "So is decorating a tree."

"Is that the night you guys do that huge bonfire thing?" Kori asked excitedly. "As a kid, I used to wonder what it would be like to be there standing right before that roaring fire."

"A lot of people are drawn to our big fire. We have to really step up security that night to keep trespassers out. It's members only."

Kori rolled her eyes in mocked solemnity. "Is that when some deep, dark, secret Wheel ritual takes place?"

"Do I have to keep telling you? We have no secrets. We're very transparent about who we are and what we believe. It's right there on our matchbooks."

"The raw food diet was a secret, though."

"And what's so bad about welcoming our guests with a feast?"

Kori patted her shoulder. "All right. I don't mean to dis your religion. How are the fries?"

"Have one." Flicker pushed the container closer to Kori. "I could get you in," she said, in a hushed, reverent tone.

It took Kori a second to realize Flicker was still talking about Winter Solstice. She'd love to see the fire, but she shuddered at the thought of stepping foot into Promisedland again. "Gee, thanks, but I can't. My dad will be home on leave then." She raised her shoulders and grinned. "I'm so excited to see him! It's been six months!"

"You can spare one night away from him. Flame was very impressed with your fund raising. She even bragged about you to Real Father."

"She did? To Promus?"

Flicker gave a confident nod. "He hasn't given up on you. I haven't either."

"I saw how Wheel of Fire treats its loyal members. That was a dirty trick Ashe played on Glow. I'll never forget the look on her face as the van pulled away."

Flicker swirled a fry in ketchup and popped it in her mouth. "She probably found her way to some homeless shelter."

"She drove there in her car?"

"Look, Kori, there's no place in God's army for deadbeats." Flicker lifted the container of fries toward her as a peace offering. Kori reached her hand out, and the fries launched into the air and rained down around them. A man gripped Flicker by the armpits and was dragging her backward off the bench. She flailed her legs, screaming, "No, Satan!"

The man clamped her mouth with his broad hand. He was muscular with bulging biceps and a beard. A taller, heavyset man grabbed her legs. Kori recognized them as the guys who were talking to Flicker in the River Park parking lot.

"Don't struggle and you won't get hurt," the fat man told her calmly.

"Ouch! God damn it! She bit me!" The bearded man turned his hand to examine his palm, which was bleeding out of two puncture wounds.

"Save me, Kori," yelled Flicker, her eyes rolling, showing mostly white.

The two men carried her to their black SUV, which had backed into a blue disabled person's parking stall. The license plate was covered in mud; Kori could only make out a 5 and a T. The door of the backseat was open, and the two men tossed Flicker in. Muscle man ran around the vehicle and jumped into the front passenger's seat next to the driver, a woman wearing a scarf and oversized sunglasses. The other guy climbed into the backseat, his arms raised to fend off Flicker's kicking feet.

Kori sat paralyzed, her jaw dropped. This was no ordinary kidnapping. What it was, she wasn't sure, but Flicker was obviously traumatized. She couldn't let her friend go through such an ordeal alone. She took a running start and dove into the backseat of the vehicle.

"Christ's sake, get out!" yelled the man next to her.

"Push her out!" said the beard from the front seat.

"There isn't time," said the driver, pulling forward.

Kori scrambled to a seated position, and the overweight man reached across her to slam the door shut. "You're making a big mistake," he warned through clenched teeth.

They passed a young mother, who was pushing a stroller and holding a toddler's hand. Her eyes and mouth were round with horror as she gawked after the speeding vehicle. A worker ran out of the restaurant and punched out three numbers on his cell: 9-1-1.

The driver took a hard right, and then swerved left onto the Highway 99 on-ramp. She sped south and turned off at the next exit, then zigzagged over country roads, running most stop signs and skidding to a crawl at blind intersections. These rough, narrow roads weren't built for speed, and Kori bounced so high that she hit her head. The man in the backseat was nearly sitting on Flicker to keep her quiet and out of sight.

"We know who you are, Kori," the man in front addressed her over the seat. "We're just not sure whose side you're on."

"Flicker's."

"We'd rather have you on Chelsea's," said the woman.

"Who's that?" Kori asked, realizing the answer before she finished speaking.

"Chelsea Cunningham." The man seated next to Kori hooked this thumb toward Flicker. "Your friend here."

So Kori had been right in identifying Flicker in the Missing Persons files! What threw her off was the age. Chelsea had been only a junior when she ran away—sixteen, seventeen at the most. She must have lied about her age when she joined the Wheel. Ha! Promus didn't know everything!

The woman pulled off the road behind a white sedan. The two men struggled to half drag, half carry Flicker into the white car. The female driver got out, so Kori did, too.

A man jumped out of the white car. "Good luck," he said, as he slipped into the SUV and drove it west on a dirt road, dust billowing behind.

"Who are you?" Kori asked the woman who dashed toward the driver's side of the white car.

"Deprogrammers, hired by Chelsea's parents. Here's where you get off."

Flicker stomped hard on the paunchy man's foot and kicked back to what she could reach, which happened to be his kneecap. He cried out, as she broke away and sprinted into a field of withered cornstalks.

"Ah, hell," said the woman. She jogged down the dirt road, and Kori followed her. In the sunlight Kori could see through the scarf that she was nearly bald, with only a few wisps of hair. The men entered the cornfield perpendicular to them to head Flicker off.

"I want to help you," Kori shouted to the woman.

"Then call someone to get a ride back to Goldhurst."

"Why can't I come with you?"

"Because kidnapping is a capital offense."

"I'm coming freely."

"She's not." The woman was staring down at Flicker, who had been tackled by the two men. "The less you know about us the better for us."

"Run, Kori!" Flicker screamed. "Call Promus! Tell him Satan's got hold of me! Tell him which way we went."

The woman extended her hand toward Kori. "I'll take your phone."

"If you'd just let me call my mom to let her know I'm okay." Kori slid her phone out of her jacket pocket.

The woman made a grab for it, and when Kori held it out of her reach, the bearded man snatched it from behind her. "Sorry. Too much of a risk."

The three deprogrammers tried to pull Flicker toward the car as she continued to struggle and scream, "Satan!"

Kori patted her shoulder. "Calm down. These people are trying to help you."

"You devil, Kori. You betrayed me *and* Real Father. God will punish you. You're in on this!"

"Flicker, I'm not!"

The men managed to load Flicker's writhing body into the car. They continued on, the driver navigating the country roads toward the freeway. In the back seat, Flicker hunched over and sobbed. Kori reached across the man between them and took her hand. Flicker squeezed it, and Kori squeezed back. Flicker rocked her body, chanting, "Come, spirit of Michael. Come, spirit of Michael."

A tractor up ahead caused the driver to slow. She craned her neck trying to see if it was clear to pass. Flicker let out a yelp, unlatched the door, and bailed. The driver skidded to a stop. Flicker rolled in and out of a ditch, scrambled to her feet, and limped through an orchard.

"Here we go again," the heavyset man said wearily.

The two men and Kori chased after Flicker. This time when they caught her, the bearded man held her down while the other one stabbed her arm with a syringe. Flicker fought her captors a few more seconds before drifting into unconsciousness.

"I really didn't want to do that," said the man who had administered the injection.

"I saw you guys in Fresno," said Kori.

"We try to talk clients into coming willfully first." The man paused, gasping for air. "It gets messy when we have to use force."

"I was so scared when Flicker jumped out of the moving vehicle," said Kori. "She could have killed herself!"

"How many times do you think she's heard Vince Dower tell her she should kill herself or others rather than leave the Wheel?" asked the shorter man.

"How do you know?" Kori asked.

"I'm Dave, an ex-Wheel member. This is Chuck and Helen. He's a psychiatrist specializing in exit-counseling, and she has a twin brother in the Wheel."

"My family has been trying to get him out for years," she said. "Ed was working on his Ph.D. when Promus got a hold of him."

"I think I know him–Stix?"

"Yeah, right." Helen pursed her lips in a sour expression.

Dave hoisted Flicker's limp body into his arms, and they walked toward the car. Kori got in the backseat, and Chuck set Flicker gently beside her before climbing in after her. Flicker slumped over, her head resting in Kori's lap.

"From the moment I saw Flick–I mean, Chelsea–I've wanted to help her get free of the Wheel."

"We've been observing you for a while. We couldn't tell if you were trying to get her out or she was trying to get you in," said Helen.

Kori sighed. "Both, I guess."

"You're playing with fire," said Dave, "no pun intended. Lots of people think they're above being recruited by a cult, then–*wham*–they're in."

"We're sorry about this, Kori," said Chuck, "but we're got to blindfold you and ask you to duck down."

The idea of the blindfold unnerved her. "Do we really have to be so dramatic?"

"Yes," said Dave. "If anyone like Vince or Sharon asks you where you've been, you honestly won't know. I don't think you realize the danger you've put yourself in."

"There's a way you don't have to wear the blindfold and can get your phone back," said Helen, glancing at Kori through the rearview mirror. "You can bail."

"I'm in," she said, determined to see Flicker through this.

Chuck tied a scarf over Kori's eyes, and she slid down in the seat. She felt helpless without her phone and disoriented under the blindfold. She was 99 percent sure she could trust these people, but it was that nagging one percent that worried her. She lay quietly, trying to figure out where they were going. It seemed like more than an hour passed. Kori could feel that they were climbing the Grapevine, heading into L.A. Then there were just too many freeway exchanges for her to keep track.

The car came to a stop, and Dave told Kori she could remove the blindfold and sit up. Her back and legs ached from her cramped position. It was dusk, and it took her eyes a few seconds to adjust to the dimness. They were parked at the rear of a large two-story motel, the name of it obscured.

Everyone got out of the car. Helen knocked on the door of one of the rooms. Kori noticed the room number, but she looked away before she could read it.

A pretty, pregnant women in her mid-twenties greeted them, introducing herself as Melanie. Her long hair was set in curls and her makeup was artfully applied. Her finger marked her place in a Bible she held.

Inside the room, Dave set Flicker in a winged chair, and Melanie sat next to her, taking her hand. Helen gave Kori a cool, wet washcloth and instructed her to talk softly to Flicker as she wiped her face and neck. In a few moments, Flicker lobbed her head back and forth and groaned. Her eyes popped open with a start. "Where am I?"

Kori made sure that her face was in the direct line of her vision. "Hi, Flicker."

"Kori?" She rubbed her forehead. "Oh! I had a nightmare. I dreamt that I had been…." A look of terror crossed her face. She tried to scramble to her feet, but Dave, standing behind her, gently but firmly held her in the chair.

"Don't, Satan!" she shouted, wheeling around to glare at him. "Don't rape and torture me!"

"No one is going to hurt you," Chuck said calmly.

Flicker dropped her face into her hands and began to rock back and forth, moaning more than singing, "Onward, Christian Soldiers."

Melanie joined in, in a sweet soprano. Flicker lifted her head, sat up, and stared at her. "Melanie?"

"Hi, Chels! Long time, no see!"

Flicker eyes swept over Melanie's full body. "You're…pregnant!"

"Yep. You're gonna be an aunt! Jack and I were married in February."

"It's too late! The Armageddon is coming! Your baby won't reach the age of reason. He won't know what side to take, and the devil will bear him away!"

"Jesus would never let that happen. See?" She opened her Bible to an illustration of Jesus seated with a group of children, a lamb lying at his feet. "On Judgment Day, which is probably thousands of years from now, Jesus will raise all the little children up into heaven with him."

"No!" said Flicker. "Promus said–"

"Vince hates kids," said Dave. "He's had a vasectomy to keep from impregnating his sex-slaves, and he makes sure they're all over eighteen so he won't get busted for statutory rape."

Flicker twisted free of Dave's grip, screaming, "Shut up, devil. Blasphemer! Tormentor! Don't touch me!"

"Oh, the baby just kicked!" Melanie exclaimed joyfully. "Would you like to feel?" She placed Flicker's hand on her abdomen.

Her eyes widened. "I do feel him!"

"Her," corrected Melanie. "That's your little niece Chelsea in there."

"Chelsea. I like that name," said Flicker. "I knew a Chelsea once."

"Your name is Chelsea," said Chuck. "Chelsea Cunningham."

"I'm Flicker," she insisted.

"You're also Chelsea," said Melanie in a soothing voice. "You're going to be Auntie Chelsea to little Chelsea here. Now, would you like to say hello to her daddy?"

"Jack's here?" asked Chelsea, looking around her.

"In the room next door," said Chuck. "We didn't want to overwhelm you with too many people at once. We can notify him if you want to see him."

"Sure, I do."

Chuck tapped a text message on his phone.

Within seconds, an energetic, lanky man entered the room.

"Jack!" Chelsea leaped from her chair and ran into his arms, the impact causing him to drop a DVD he was holding. Brother and sister hugged a long time.

"It's great to see you, Chels," said Jack. "Sorry you couldn't be at the wedding. Melanie wanted you to sing."

"I never knew about it," said Flicker/Chelsea.

"We sent you a wedding invitation," said Jack.

"I never got it," said Flicker/Chelsea.

"Well, you did take a Shunning Vow against us," Jack reminded her.

Flicker nodded solemnly. "I shouldn't be talking to you now."

"Me? Your own brother?"

"Promus is my Real Father. The Wheel is my family," she recited hypnotically.

"A short visit can't hurt." Jack picked up the DVD. "I brought something to show you."

"Your wedding?" asked Chelsea.

"You'll see." Jack inserted the DVD into the player and turned on the TV.

At first Kori didn't recognize her. She was watching a pretty, younger Chelsea, dressed in a cowgirl's outfit, singing and dancing on a stage, "Anything you can do, I can do better."

Flicker watched for a while. "Oh, she's good."

"That's you!" said Jack. "Chelsea Cunningham, star of Pacific High's production, *Annie Get Your Gun.*"

Chelsea gazed at the video until a tear trickled down her nose. "That was a really fun show."

"You can have that life back, Chels," said Jack. "You can go live with Mom and Dad while you get your GED and apply to colleges. You've got your whole life ahead of you."

"Are you going to waste it on Vincent Dower?" asked Dave. "I used to be just like you, doing everything he said, eating raw food, exercising in the middle of the night, begging in the streets, chanting and squeezing people's hands. Vince gets you so exhausted and hungry you can't think straight. He is not a prophet. He's a deranged megalomaniac who gets his power by controlling his followers."

"Satan!" Flicker sprinted toward the door, but Chuck and Helen barred her way. She tried to dive through the window, but Dave stopped her. She ran toward the bathroom, but Jack stood in her path.

She turned to Kori, tears streaming downing her face. "Kori, won't you save me?"

"I'm trying," she said gently.

Flicker plopped into her seat and began rocking back and forth, chanting, "Come, Michael, come, Michael," in a rapid, agitated voice.

Chuck sent another text. A middle-aged couple entered the room. The man was athletic and tall with gray hair, his tan face creased with concern. The woman was dressed in slacks, a cashmere sweater, and a gold cross.

"My Sea-sea," she murmured, silent tears dripping down her face. "My baby girl."

"Hello, honey," said Mr. Cunningham. "We've missed you so much."

Chelsea abruptly stopped chanting and looked up. "Mom? Dad?"

They hugged in a group, Melanie and Jack joining the huddle.

Kori thought Promus's hold on Chelsea had been broken, but then Flicker said, "It's great to see you all, but I've got to get back to Promisedland. By now I've been missed."

Chuck bent to look into Flicker's face. "Chelsea, listen. I'm here to help you make the transition back to your own life."

"Wheel of Fire is my life! Promus is my Real Father!"

"That's what you've been brainwashed to believe, Chelsea," said Chuck. "I want you to give me some time to present you with some alternative ideas. If your faith in Promus is strong, it won't matter what we tell you."

"How much time?" asked Flicker/Chelsea.

"Five days."

"And then I can return to Promidedland?"

"If that's what you want, honey," said Mr. Cunningham. "I'll drive you there myself."

Flicker/Chelsea sighed. "Can we go home, Mom? I mean, um, to your house? I'd like to see my old room."

"If that's what you want to do after five days, Chelsea," said Chuck. "Until then we're staying here, on neutral ground."

"Oh, Chelsea! Why did you run away?" asked Mrs. Cunningham. "Did we do something?"

Chelsea swiped at her tears with the back of her hand and looked down at her lap. "No." she said finally. "It was Tristan and Taylor. I wanted to hurt them."

"Who are they?" Kori asked.

A flash of indignation crossed Melanie's face. "Tristan was her boyfriend. He dumped her then asked her best friend to the junior prom."

Chelsea stared at a spot on the carpet. "I couldn't face them. I couldn't go back to school. I knew all the kids were laughing at me."

"You hurt us so much," exclaimed Mrs. Cunningham.

"It was all part of God's plan," said Flicker. "It's how I came to Real Father."

"Oh, I don't think a child running away from good parents is ever a part of God's plan," said Melanie.

Flicker didn't seem to hear her. Chelsea looked at her mom. "Are they still together?"

"No. Tristan went away to college, and Taylor's still in town, going to the community college and bagging groceries. She asks me about you every time I see her."

"It wasn't Taylor's fault," said Chelsea. "Tristan was such an asshole."

Everyone burst out laughing. Chelsea looked at the circle of people around her and smiled through her tears.

There was a discussion about dinner, and Flicker/Chelsea asked for her favorite, sweet and sour pork. Jack called in an order of Chinese food, and he and Melanie went to pick it up. While they were waiting for the food to arrive, Flicker/Chelsea stretched out on one of the beds.

"I'm so tired. I think I'll just rest here a moment." In minutes she was asleep.

When the food arrived, Chuck suggested that they let her sleep. "We'll be sure she gets plenty of rest the next five days. Her situation may appear a lot different to her when she's not sleep-deprived."

Kori told the Cunninghams how she had met Flicker and all that she knew about her life in the Wheel, while Chuck took notes. She turned to Helen, "I better get going. Can I call my mom now?"

Helen shook her head. "I'll drive you to a place where someone can pick you up."

Mrs. Cunningham hugged her good-bye. "Thank you for being such a good friend to Chelsea."

Kori walked to the bed, bent over Flicker/Chelsea and stroked her matted hair. "Good-bye, Chelsea," she whispered. "I hope you find your way back to your real life."

Melanie held up crossed fingers. "So far, so good!"

Outside the motel room, Helen instructed Kori to get in the backseat and lie down. She handed her the blindfold over the car seat.

"Again?" Kori protested.

She nodded. "For our protection and yours."

They drove for over an hour. Helen pulled into a gas station and told Kori she could remove the blindfold. She slid it off and sat up. They were in Santa Clarita, across the highway from Magic Mountain. They got gas, used the restroom, and bought drinks. Helen let Kori sit up front, and they were on their way again.

Kori smiled to herself, visualizing Flicker/Chelsea's sweet face as she talked to her family members. Her mom was going to ground her for life, but it was worth it. She had seen Chelsea home. "It seems like Chelsea's deprogramming is going to take more like five hours than five days."

"Don't underestimate Promus's grip on her. We've tried to deprogram Ed a couple of times." Helen touched her scarf. "There was a time when I wasn't sure I'd survive cancer. My dying wish was to see Ed free from the Wheel."

"How long has he been involved?"

"He was one of the originals back in Wyoming. He meant to go to Eden only for the summer. It was just a commune at first—no religion, just people who wanted to drop out for a while. Ed was stuck on his dissertation and went there to think."

"How long ago was that?"

"Twelve years," said Helen, with a shake of her head. "Ed and I will turn thirty-seven next month."

"And Stix—I mean Ed—believes the angel story?"

"Totally."

"But he's so smart! So…scientific!"

"I know. I think he panicked. He was afraid his committee would never pass his dissertation so to avoid academic embarrassment he followed Vince like a blind sheep."

As they climbed the Grapevine heading out of L.A., Kori noticed the roadside AMBER alert signs were lit:

CHILD ABDUCTION
BLACK SUV
CA LICENSE 5T 6
1 800 TELL CHP

How tragic it was that some poor parents were missing their child, who had possibly been kidnapped. Helen drove by three more of the informational signs before Kori slapped her palm to her mouth. "That child is me!"

Helen smiled wryly. "Yeah. You were an unnecessary complication, Kori, but I think you did help."

"Who owns the black SUV?"

"We do. My husband won't be happy that part of our license plate is up there on the AMBER alert signs."

"Was he the guy who drove off?"

She nodded. "He's a reluctant participant. It's not always easy for him to understand my obsession with getting Ed and other victims out of the Wheel."

After they descended into California's Central Valley, Helen returned Kori's phone and dropped her off in Grapevine, a little town of fast food restaurants and gas stations. When Kori turned on her phone, a flurry of text messages appeared, most of them from her mom and Luke. She went into the McDonald's and called her mom.

"I'm okay," Kori blurted as soon as she answered. "I need you to come pick me up in Grapevine."

"Kori! I've been going nuts! Witnesses said you were carried off by two men, kicking and screaming."

"That was Flicker. Chelsea, I mean. The girl in Wheel of Fire. Those guys are deprogrammers. Sorry to cause you so much worry."

Kori texted Luke: "I'm okay."

"You were kidnapped?????"

"No. I'll explain when I C U."

"When?"

"Tonight. I'll text U when I can."

Kori expected to wait over an hour, but in less than five minutes, a California Highway Patrol cruiser pulled up, its blue lights flashing. Somehow she knew it was her ride. The CHP radioed in that he had found her, and it wasn't long after that that the AMBER alerts went black.

The officer drove Kori to the Goldhurst Police Department, where TV, radio, and newspaper reporters waited in front of the building. As the officer escorted Kori to the door, the media people flocked around her, sticking microphones in her face and asking questions. She muttered,

"No comment." Once she was inside the building, she was led into Officer Huerta's office where her mom was waiting.

After a lot of hugging alternating with scolding from them both, Kori sat down and told the whole story.

"I still can't believe you got into that SUV," Officer Huerta exclaimed, typing up her report. "You're one reckless girl."

Cindy pressed her fingers to her temples. "I can't believe any of this. What if those people really were kidnappers? You took a tremendous risk, Kori, and for what?"

"Oh, Mom, I really wanted to help Chelsea."

"Well, now that your friend is home safe with her family, this should be the end of this Wheel business. Finally."

Kori nodded, but she was thinking of Luke's mom. Her phone chimed to announce an incoming text.

It was from Luke: "Are U back? Im at the diner."

Kori looked up at her mom with pleading eyes. "It's Luke. Is it okay if I go have coffee with him at Main Street Diner?"

"Go ahead. But hurry home, and don't get into anymore trouble tonight."

Outside on the street, she broke into a run, pumping her legs high, occasionally leaping with joy. Flicker—Chelsea—was free!

She spotted Luke standing in front of the diner, and she dashed toward him. His arms were tightly crossed, when she was expecting a big hug.

"I just don't understand you sometimes, Kori."

"Oh, you're mad. Please don't be angry, babe." She held his chin in her fingertips, moving in for a kiss.

He jerked away. "Why the fuck would you jump into a car with strangers?"

"I just had a feeling they were okay, you know?"

"No, I don't know! Witnesses said they were violently, *violently* attacking Flicker, and you just went along with them. They could have been anybody—like enemies of Promus out to get him through you girls."

"Promus has enemies?"

"I don't know. Come on." He put his arm around her waist and kissed the top of her head. "Crazy stupid," he whispered in her ear, and nipped her lobe.

Seated in the restaurant, Luke reached his hands across the table to grasp Kori's. "I wish you'd just leave it. Forget the Wheel exists."

"Your mother's trapped in it. Are we supposed to forget about her, too?"

He shrugged. "She forgot about us."

"She didn't, babe. You should have seen the way she stared at your photo when I handed it to her. She just needs our help getting her out. Those deprogrammers were amazing! Totally effective."

"You don't know that yet. Flicker could still return to the Wheel."

Kori shook her head. "Chelsea. This could work with your mom. We could plan an intervention!"

Luke looked uncertain. "What sort of intervention?"

"I was thinking about it on my way back from L.A. Your mom is in charge of gathering, and I can offer her our pomegranates."

"I thought they were dead."

"Just diseased. They're good for juicing. Anyway, when her picking crew comes over, I'll find an excuse to get her into my house, and there will be the deprogrammer and your whole family." Kori snapped her fingers. "We got her!"

"Whoa! Whoa!" Luke held up his palms. "I have a feeling my dad won't go for this."

"Why not? He wants your mom back, doesn't he?"

Luke took a deep breath and exhaled, his chest heaving. "I really don't know. He's pretty bitter about the whole thing. You expect my mom to return home after two years and then just pick up her life where she left it off like nothing ever happened?"

She bit her lower lip as she smiled. "Something like that."

"Kori." He just shook his head.

"Luke!" She pumped his hands up and down. "You want her back." She pumped again. "The kids want her back." Another shake. "Your dad will just have to take her back!" A glimmer appeared in Luke's eyes, and she gave his hands a final bounce. "Let's break her out!"

Chapter Twelve

Kori was in her economics class, and the lunch bell was about to ring. She tried to focus as her teacher explained the homework, but she was distracted by the fact that this was the fifth day of Flicker's deprogramming. Tomorrow she would decide to stay with her family and resume her life as Chelsea Cunningham or return to Wheel of Fire as Flicker.

An office aide entered the classroom with a hall pass for her. It said that she was excused from class a few minutes early because her dad was here to take her to lunch. *Her dad*? So the reason he had never given her the details of his flight was because he wanted to surprise her! In just a few minutes, she would be hugging her own dear daddy!

Kori packed up with shaking fingers, scurried out of class and across campus, texting Luke as she went: "Cant make lunch. Call U later." She stepped into the school office and halted, her mouth dropping open in disbelief. The man waiting there, dressed in a US Army camouflage uniform, was not her dad.

Promus flashed his leering grin at the school secretary. "Told you she'd be surprised." He pressed his hand between Kori's shoulder blades and steered her out the door.

Do something! Scream! Run! But what would the office help think? Kori didn't want to cause a scene. She tried to speak, to tell Promus she didn't want to go with him, but her tongue seemed locked in place. She tried to stop walking, but her feet automatically moved forward. In the parking lot, he opened the passenger side of a black Mercedes sedan, and she slid in. He got in the driver's seat.

"Where…where are we going?" Kori croaked, forcing her mouth into motion.

He laughed. "To lunch, honey. Do you think I would lie to your nice school secretary?"

He drove to *Casa de Uvas*, the most expensive restaurant in Goldhurst. Kori had never been there. The maître d' greeted Promus as "Mr. Dower," and led them through the dimly lit main dining area to a back room where the tables were partitioned off in private alcoves. A waiter handed them two-foot high menus and retreated.

"They serve raw food here?" Kori asked.

"What do you mean?" replied Promus, as playful as a cat about to pounce on a mouse.

"Wheel of Fire members eat only raw food."

He waved away the comment. "That's all Sharon's doing. She always was a health food nut. She isn't here, is she?" He pressed his forefinger to his lips. "Shh! Don't tell!" From his satchel, he removed a bronze fire dish, placed it in the center of the table, and lit it. He ordered for them both without asking Kori what she wanted. When her Lobster Thermidor was served, she could hardly force it down. She thought about Flicker and the other Wheel members begging in the pouring rain and eating nuts and seeds.

"Food good?" Promus asked.

Kori nodded. "Why did you lie about being my dad?"

"So I could release you from school."

"Why? Why am I here?"

"To have lunch, of course." He seemed to be thoroughly enjoying himself, sniffing, swirling, and downing some expensive wine.

Minutes passed when there was no sound but the clinking of their forks. Finally he shoved aside his plate and leaned toward Kori. "I want to personally thank you for trying to prevent Flicker's abduction."

Did he really believe that was her intention? "Uh, I wasn't much help, really," Kori replied cautiously, watching his face.

"You were brave, my daughter, jumping into that van, sticking with her like that. The poor girl was terrified. She would have died of fright if it weren't for you. Where did they take her?"

"Somewhere in L.A. I was blindfolded."

"Her parents' house?"

"No. A motel room."

"What motel, what city?"

"I don't know."

The muscles in his face twitched in annoyance, but his tone remained controlled. "What was the room number?"

Kori shrugged.

He slammed his hand down, causing the fire dish to jump. "Any idiot would have noticed that!"

"I guess I'm not an idiot then."

He grinned. His teeth looked large and square and fierce. "No, my daughter, you certainly aren't. There were two men and a woman, right? What did they call each other? Don't protect these people, Kori. They work for Satan. Was one named Dave? The others Charles and Helen?"

She lowered her eyes.

"Look at me, Kori Lawton!" His breath caused the flame to waver dangerously over the tablecloth.

Her eyes unwillingly met his. She felt her chin bob uncontrollably.

His expression was as beatific as the Buddha. "That's all I need to know. Bless you, my daughter. May Michael's spirit enflame your soul."

Promus ordered them coffee and key lime pie, but the thought of another bite sickened her. She had betrayed Dave, Chuck, and Helen just as they feared she might.

"I don't know why I care if I get Flicker back," he said abruptly.

"She's devoted to you!"

"True, but her spirit is weak. Not like yours, Kori Lawton. I've got plans for you."

"I'm not interested in joining the Wheel. I don't believe any of what you–"

"You will, my daughter, you will." He shot her his wide-eyed look of inner wisdom. "You're going to be of great service."

She met his stare, even though her eyes smarted like peering through smoke. He was not handsome, she decided, but she could see how he attracted other women.

"I hear you've invited Ember and her committee to visit your home this weekend."

"Yes, to gather our pomegranates."

"How generous of you, daughter, to offer sustenance to my poor, needy family."

Kori ignored his sarcasm, which might suggest he knew she had an ulterior motive. "Our crop isn't suitable for market this year, but Ember can juice them."

"She'll be grateful for that, poor Ember. She does her best to feed us, but you know what kind of fire an ember is?" He shook his head. "Dying."

"I heard her coughing at the service. She's really sick."

"I'm doing what I can for her."

The longer Kori was with Promus, the braver she became in speaking up. "Faith healing doesn't really work."

"It can if people believe it does." He touched his temple. "Never underestimate the power of the mind. Ember is quite obstinate, you know. Weak in her faith."

"She needs to see a doctor."

"I don't believe one could help her. Ember came to us in a very weakened condition, the mother of seven needy brats who nearly sucked the marrow out of her bones."

Kori's face flushed. Did he know Luke was her boyfriend, and that he had come looking for her in Promisedland? He must. He knew everything else about her.

Promus paid with an American Express card bearing the name Vincent E. Dower. He dropped Kori back at school just before the late bell sounded. Shaken, slumped against the front gate pole, she watched the black Mercedes disappear out of sight. Her dad had not returned to her after all. Promus had tricked her. Then he had wrung her dry.

The ding of an incoming text brought her back to the present. "Waz up?" Luke asked.

She would have to lie to him. Again. It made her skin crawl to be in the presence of Promus, and yet she had walked with him to his car, gotten in, and allowed herself to be driven off. How could she explain to Luke that she had gone to lunch with Promus against her will when she couldn't even explain it to herself?

Throughout the week, Kori and Luke worked on the details of their intervention. When she told her mom their plan, Cindy welcomed Luke and his mom into their home, but Kori had to do some fast-talking to get her to allow the Wheel of Fire gatherers on their property. Kori and Luke needed professional help, but they didn't know how to contact Dave or Helen. Searching the Internet, Kori discovered that Chuck was actually Dr. Charles Willets. She also learned that exit counselors charged thousands of dollars. Luke thought of a source of free counseling, Matt Schuller, the pastor at Valley Community Church. Finally, they were ready to approach Luke's dad with their plans. Luke told him that he had invited Kori to dinner Wednesday night because they had something important to discuss with him.

Kori arrived early and helped Luke make spaghetti, salad, and garlic bread. Dinner at the Jamison's was the usual chaos, with Annie complaining she didn't like anything, Connor being sullen and withdrawn, and little Billy and Lizzie making a mess of their food. Mr. Jamison didn't have much to say. He kept sneaking furtive glances at Kori's abdomen. At first she thought she had spilled something on her shirt. She was shocked to realize that he probably thought Luke and she were about to tell him she was pregnant!

Kori helped Luke clean up the kitchen while Mr. Jamison put Billy and Lizzie to bed. Annie read to Kori in the living room, sounding quite advanced for a first grader, while at the kitchen table, Luke went over some math problems with Connor, who didn't seem to be paying attention in class. After Connor and Annie went to bed, Mr. Jamison, Luke, and Kori sat down to coffee in the living room.

Mr. Jamison looked solemn, fearing bad news. "What's this about, kids?" The doorbell rang, startling him. He shifted his eyes to the front door. "Are you expecting someone, Luke?"

"I asked Pastor Schuller to drop by."

"Oh, Lord," Mr. Jamison muttered.

Luke answered the door. The pastor was a clean-cut young guy, dressed in jeans and a plaid, button-down shirt. He shook hands with Mr. Jamison. "Hi, Andy. It's been a while."

"I know, Matt. Hello."

"This is Kori," said Luke, and she shook hands with the pastor. Luke served him coffee. There was an uncomfortable silence.

"Kori?" Luke prompted.

She took a deep breath and launched into her pitch. "Well, I want to help your family get Mrs. Jamison out of Wheel of Fire."

Mr. Jamison dropped his head and rubbed his brow. "Oh, no," he groaned.

"Wait!" Kori talked faster. "I met a girl who was in the Wheel. She invited me to a few services, and we got to be friends. I took part in a deprogramming intervention for her, and it made me hope we could do something like that for Mrs. Jamison."

"The deprogramming was a success?" asked Pastor Schuller.

"It was easy! My friend's family just reminded her what her life had been like before she entered the Wheel, and they all showed her how much they love her. So here's what I'm thinking for Ember–I mean, Mrs. Jamison…" Kori was breathless, her heart racing.

"Nearly two years have gone by," Mr. Jamison stated flatly. "This family has moved on. We've had to."

"Please, listen to our plan," Kori said. "Mrs. Jamison and some other Wheel members are coming over to our ranch Saturday morning to pick pomegranates. I'm going to think of an excuse for her to come into the house, and there, sitting in our living room, will be you guys and all the kids. We should try to get Terry and Gracie to come, too."

Mr. Jamison sighed. "I appreciate what you're trying to do, Kori, but you don't understand the situation. I don't want my children to see that their mother has become a pathetic robot. Billy and Lizzie don't even remember her, and Connor and Anne…well, I don't know what they think, but it wouldn't do them any good to know their mother lives in the area, but won't have anything to do with them."

"But if she sees them, she'll want to come home to them," Kori insisted.

"No," said Mr. Jamison. "She has to leave the Wheel on her own accord, and if she wants to live here again with us…that's a whole other can of worms."

"What if you talk to her, Pastor Schuller?" Kori asked. "Luke told me she was really active in your church."

He cleared his throat. "I'd like to help, but I agree with Andy. These interventions seldom work. It will have to be Maureen's idea. Right now, she's brainwashed into believing Promus's dogma of faith rather than ours."

"That part of it may not be so." Mr. Jamison thoughtfully rubbed the stubble on his chin.

"I know what you mean!" Kori exclaimed. "She doesn't seem that into Promus, not like the others."

"All I know is when Promus pressured her to get a divorce, she refused him," said Mr. Jamison.

"She must believe what Promus preaches." Pastor Schuller leaned forward. "Why else would she be there?"

"I've asked myself the same question a hundred times," said Mr. Jamison. "One day she just left our little ones unsupervised and made a beeline for that cult, like a woman possessed."

"But she won't get a divorce," Luke reminded his dad.

"Well, she doesn't hate us. Your mother knows divorce would bring financial ruin to this family. I'd have to sell everything and give her half. This land has been in my family for generations. I could never afford to replace it at today's prices."

"And you know who would get Mom's share," Luke said bitterly.

Mr. Jamison smiled at Kori with bloodshot eyes. "You're a real spunky gal. I bet your daddy is mighty proud of you."

If he was, he hadn't indicated it lately. Her dad still hadn't firmed up his plans for his Christmas leave. Kori threw up her hands and let them drop with a slap on her thighs. "So that's it? None of you want to even try to get Mrs. Jamison back? I'm in this alone?"

"I'm in," said Luke. "I'd like to see Mom again, even if this intervention thing doesn't work."

"I'll be happy to talk to her if she wants," said Pastor Schuller, "but she has to come to me."

The minister left soon after that. When Luke walked Kori to her truck, he kissed her good-night and held her in his arms a long while.

"I'm not gonna lie, babe," he whispered in her ear. "I'm scared to get my hopes up."

Kori flattened her hands against his chest to look into his expressive eyes, so much like Ember's. "This *will* work, Luke! We're gonna get your mom back!"

Chapter Thirteen

Luke was wearing out the carpet pacing in circles, his arms folded tightly across his chest. "She isn't coming. She's been tipped off."

Kori pulled Luke's arms to his sides and looked into his troubled countenance. "Chill! It's not even nine o'clock."

They heard a vehicle pull into the driveway, and both of them dashed to the window to find an orange Wheel of Fire van.

"See? What'd I tell you?" Kori ran out the back door to greet the Wheelers, six of them including Ember, carrying burlap sacks.

"Hi, guys, follow me." Kori led them down the driveway and around the garage, then pointed toward the pomegranate orchards. "The skins are discolored, but the fruit is just fine."

As the Wheel's picking crew walked on, Kori caught Ember's elbow. "Can you come in the house a minute? My mom wants to meet you."

She stopped, her brow creased. "Whatever for?"

"Well, she went to high school with Mr. Jamison, and I am dating Luke, and—"

"That has nothing to do with me."

"I know, but I just thought…okay, I'm the one who wants you to meet my mom. I want her to see…I want her to know you're—"

"Not crazy?"

"…doing fine."

Ember broke into a fit of coughing, causing her to double over.

"Come on. I'll get you some water." Kori led her through the back door and pulled out a kitchen chair for her. Ember drank from the water glass Kori offered her, and in a few minutes she breathed easier.

"Better?"

Ember nodded. "Thank you."

"You need to see a doctor, Mom." Luke appeared at the entryway between the kitchen and living room.

"Hello, Luke." She gazed over at him, her face void of expression, and then it crumpled as she hacked violently. She wheezed, struggling to clear her lungs to take her next breath. She reached into the folds of her long skirt and pulled out a white handkerchief, then spit blood-streaked mucus into it. She wiped her mouth and asked Luke in a flat tone, "Are the rest of you going to file in now? Is that your plan?"

"No, Mom. It's just me."

Ember leaned to peer behind him as if she didn't believe him. "How is everyone?"

"Dad is real sad without you."

"More like angry, I'll bet."

Luke ventured a few steps into the kitchen and leaned against the refrigerator, his arms clenched across his body. "Annie still dreams about you and wakes up in the night crying."

"And Lizzie doesn't even remember me," Ember mused.

"She's getting big. Talks a blue streak. You should hear her. Billy is a roughneck, a bully at his preschool. They need you, Mom. We all want you to come home."

Ember face softened. "You're a big help to your dad, Luke, aren't you? And Terry and Gracie, too."

Luke shook his head. "Aunt Mary is raising them."

Ember's spine tensed. "But why?"

"She offered to take them in, and they wanted to go."

"And spilt up the family? My sister has all the wrong values! She'll teach them clothes and makeup are the most important things in life. Tell your dad they need to be home."

"Why don't you tell him?" asked Luke.

"I––I, well, I just can't believe your dad would let Mary––"

A sharp rap on the back door interrupted Ember. It was probably the other Wheelers looking for her, preventing her from breaking the Rule of the Four Horsemen.

Kori went to stall them. Through the window, she spied Vaughn, wearing a goofy grin and holding something behind his back. She opened the door a crack and peered around him. He shifted his body, but not before Kori glimpsed an armful of mistletoe. It grew forty or fifty feet up in the oak trees around the property, and he had had to risk breaking his neck to get it. He was probably planning to hold it over Cindy's head as an excuse to kiss her. It was corny and stupid, and yet Kori knew her dad would never bother to make such a fuss over her.

"Mom's not here," Kori told him.

"'Course she is. Her car's here."

"We've got company."

Vaughn's eyes narrowed. He must've taken the back roads and not noticed the orange Wheel of Fire van parked in front of the house. His tone took on an indignant edge. "Guess I'll just have to introduce myself to the *company*." He pushed his way past Kori, tossed the soggy mistletoe on the kitchen counter, and stopped short before Ember. "Well, well, if it isn't Maureen Finley Jamison. Howdy doody." He tipped his cap to her.

"You two know each other?" Kori asked.

"Oh, yeah. We go way back to Porterville Elementary. Don't we, Maureen? Scuttlebutt is that you joined that fire-worshipping cult. Whatcha doin' here? Goin' door-to-door peddling your little matchbooks?"

"She's here to visit her son," said Kori.

Ember gathered her skirt. "I need to go find the others."

"The others?" Vaughn raised his eyebrows. "You're letting those fire-starters overrun the place, Kori? Quick, grab the fire extinguisher and go on after them."

Ember stood to confront him. "You don't know a thing about it, Vaughn, but that's never stopped you from mouthing off."

He hooked his thumbs on his belt loops and rocked back on his heels. "Smartest girl in the class. How'd you ever fall for the bullshit that scalawag Promus preaches?"

Ember bolted through the back door.

"Don't go, Ember! Mrs. Jamison, wait!" Kori called after her. The door slammed, and she turned on Vaughn. "Look what you did!"

"I was only trying to help her see–"

"Next time, don't help!" Kori glared at him, her face twisted with all the disgust she felt for him.

Vaughn pursed his lips and blinked hard. He reeled around her and stalked through the house. "Cindy?" he called. "You know what's going on out here?"

Luke stuffed his hands in his front pockets and hung his head. "I didn't think it would work."

Kori stomped up to him. "And I have had enough of that kind of talk. Flicker got out of the Wheel, and we're springing *your mother*!" She poked him twice on his breastbone, emphasizing her last two words.

"Ow!" He rubbed his chest, gazing back at Kori in amused admiration.

Another Wheel of Fire van pulled into the driveway. Kori drew back the curtain to see the elderly sisters Roberta Frick and Rayann Malloy climb out. Right behind them was a familiar, skinny girl.

"No!" Kori yelled. "Oh, hell, no!" She dashed out the back door and down the drive.

Flicker's smile faded when she saw the anger in Kori face. She grabbed a burlap bag from the van, and scurried along with the other Wheelers, her eyes cast to the ground. As the group walked down the dirt road toward the orchard, Kori fell in step with her, seizing her arm and slowing her so that they could talk in private.

"What are you doing here, *Chelsea*?" Kori hissed through clenched teeth.

"I'm Flicker." Flustered, she shook her arm free.

"I thought you'd gone home for good to be with your family."

"Wheel of Fire is my—"

"Shut up! Shut up!" Kori clapped her palms to her ears.

"Ah, don't be mad," Flicker whined apologetically. "It was great to see Mom and Dad and everybody again. And here's the good news! My family approves of me being in the Wheel now."

"No, they don't."

"They do! They said it's my life, and I can live it as I choose. That means I don't have to shun them! I've got the best of both worlds now! I'll be granted leave to go visit when Jack and Melanie have their baby, but right now I'm back home in Promisedland with my dear Real Father just in time for Winter Solstice."

"Bonfire night?"

Flicker chuckled. "If you want to call it that. Come be my guest."

"No, thanks." Kori held up her palm.

"You said you've always wanted to see the big fire. Lots of people do and aren't allowed in. You're my best friend, and I haven't had a best friend since forever!" She was looking at Kori with those cute, crinkling eyes, expecting something back.

"I haven't had a best friend either, not since Bitsy dumped me. Well, no one, except Luke."

"He's your boyfriend! Every girl needs a *girl* best friend."

Kori nodded. "True that."

Flicker jumped up and down, clapping her hands. "Say you'll come to Winter Solstice! We'd have so much fun hanging out."

Kori imagined herself in the black winter chill, standing before the biggest fire of her life. "No," she murmured reluctantly. "I can't."

The following afternoon, all the officers on duty were out on patrol except Officer Huerta, who was in the police station with her Explorers. They were gathered in the staff lounge wrapping presents, which they were going to distribute to poor families in the community. The Explorers had brought homemade cookies, chips, and soda. "Rockin' around the Christmas Tree" was blaring on the radio. They were looking over the donated toys and talking about the best things they had gotten for Christmas when they were little.

Suddenly, the conversation and laughter stopped, and most of the kids were staring at the doorway. Kori turned to see what was wrong. Promus stood there with Flicker, her head hanging, her stringy hair flopping before her face.

Officer Huerta walked up to them. "Can I help you?"

Promus nudged Flicker. "You may speak."

She hesitated.

"Go on, my daughter," he urged gently, catching a strand of her hair and looping it behind her ear. "You'll be rewarded for this."

Flicker looked up, her voice not much more than a whisper. "I'm here to report an abduction."

"Of who?" Huerta asked.

"Me."

"Step into my office. I'll take the report."

"Kori comes, too," said Promus. "She's our best witness."

"You have no legal obligation to do this," Huerta said. "My advice would be–"

"I'll come," Kori said decisively.

They settled in chairs around Officer Huerta's desk. Promus sat close to Flicker, his arm around her shoulders. In a soft, hesitant tone, she reported the black SUV driving into the In-N-Out parking lot and two men forcing her into the vehicle, driven by a woman. "Kori jumped into the car, too," she added.

"Kori is strong in spirit," said Promus. "She tried to save Flicker."

"Let Kori speak for herself," said Huerta.

"It's true I wanted to help Flicker," Kori said, "but I never felt I was in any danger."

"That's insane!" Promus shot her a withering look. "You can't always expect Michael the Archangel to protect you, my daughter. You step in front of a speeding train or jump into a car of desperate criminals, you might not be spared."

"I'm not your daughter," Kori said, but her voice was raspy, and she couldn't lift her eyes to meet Promus's steady gaze.

Officer Huerta continued to tap the keys of her computer. "Can you describe the people in the car?" she asked Flicker.

"Their names are David Morton, Helen Kurtz, and Dr. Charles Willets," Promus stated authoritatively. "Willets is a big-time operator. He's made a fortune abducting people and brainwashing them. He's tried to steal my children from me before."

"You've got kids?" asked Officer Huerta, her wry smile challenging him. She didn't seem to have any trouble looking him straight in the eye.

"See here, I'm tired of being harassed!" Promus snapped. "I'm pressing charges this time."

"I thought Flicker was pressing charges," said Huerta.

"Right." Promus stroked Flicker's head, softly coaching her. "Tell the cop what you told me, how you were tortured, burned with cigarettes."

He addressed Huerta, "Willets uses the same brainwashing tactics as the North Koreans did in the war."

"Show me where you were burned, Flicker," said Officer Huerta.

She pushed up the sleeve of her frayed sweater to expose the inside of her wrist, pale with tiny blue veins.

"I don't see any burn marks," said Huerta.

"Real Father healed me," said Flicker.

"That's right, baby." Promus took Flicker's hand and held it in his lap. "Go on, my daughter. Who else are you pressing charges against?"

"I don't want—"

"Go on!" His tone was calm, but firm. He began to squeeze her hand in rhythmic pulses.

"Mr. and Mrs. Theodore Cunningham," she muttered, her eyes welling up.

"Your parents?" Kori asked in amazement.

Tears spurted onto Chelsea/Flicker's cheeks.

"I'm her parent," claimed Promus.

Officer Huerta completed her report. She read it aloud and asked Flicker to sign it. Her hand trembled so that she couldn't hold the pen. "My burns!" she exclaimed. "They hurt too much."

"You are weak in spirit!" Promus scolded.

Flicker shook her head, her hair flopping forward. "I'm not," she moaned.

He held the pen upright and formed her fingers around it. He withdrew his hand, and Flicker signed the report in cramped, shaky writing.

Promus stalked to the door. "Flicker, come!" He slapped his thigh as if he were calling a dog.

She scurried out after him.

Chapter Fourteen

Kori had a lot of reading to do for AP Lit over winter break, but every time she opened Dante's *Inferno*, her eyes gazed over. Christmas was only a week away, and she still hadn't heard from her dad about his leave plans.

She couldn't even hang out with Luke. He had gone with his family to Stockton to visit his grandparents for the week. To fill up the time, Kori watched her favorite old Christmas movies: *It's a Wonderful Life, Prancer, Home Alone, Miracle on 34th Street, A Christmas Story.* She imaged her own family in a feel-good movie, scenes of her dad walking in the door Christmas morning, arms outstretched to embrace her and her mom, Jared speeding up the drive in his souped-up Camaro, sprung from prison due to falsified evidence, and Vaughn slinking out the back door and out of their lives.

Reality was the opposite of her daydreams. Vaughn ate dinner with Cindy and Kori every night now. During dessert on Wednesday, he slapped an envelope addressed "Cindy and Kori" on the table.

"What's this?" asked Cindy, a smile flickering at the corners of her mouth.

"Early Christmas present. Open it, Kori."

She didn't want to be rude, but she didn't want any gift from Vaughn. She slid it near Cindy. "You do it, Mom."

Inside the envelope was a picture of a snow-covered cabin.

"It's a rental, up at Shaver Lake. I got it for us for two nights—the twenty-first and the twenty-second—plus lift tickets for both days," said Vaughn excitedly.

"I love the snow," exclaimed Cindy, "but I haven't been on skis in years."

"I'll give you a few pointers, while Kori is tearing up the mountain on her snowboard."

"We can't go!" Kori blurted. "Dad might come home then, and he'll find an empty house."

"Kori," Cindy said gently, "We would have heard from your dad by now if he was planning—"

"We might still," she insisted. "If he's not coming, he'll at least tell us. He probably can't get through on the satellite phone."

Vaughn tapped the contents of the envelope. "All of this is nonrefundable. I just assumed you were free."

"We are!" Cindy said brightly. "I'd love to go."

"Count me out!" Kori rose from the table so suddenly the plates jumped. "I don't want to be a third wheel." She knew she was acting out, but she couldn't help it. Leaving the dishes, she stalked through the house to her room and firmly shut the door.

After two days of further discussion, arguments, and tears, Cindy decided to go with Vaughn to Shaver Lake without Kori. The morning of their departure, Cindy pleaded with her one more time. "Kori, are you sure you won't come? Vaughn picked this vacation because he knows how much you love snowboarding. What are you going to do rattling around the house all by yourself?"

"I may not be by myself." Kori said adamantly. "I expect to hear from Dad any time."

"We'll be home in the early afternoon on the twenty-third. Keep your cell on, will you?"

"Sure, Mom. I'll be fine."

As soon as they left, Kori got out cookie-making ingredients, slamming the flour and sugar canisters onto the counter, and then glaring at them. She didn't have the heart to go through the process of baking alone. When she was growing up, the whole family had joined in; even Jared and her dad had decorated a few cookies. Already she regretted not going with her mom and Vaughn. She pictured herself soaring down the wintry slopes in the fresh, cold air, leaving all her cares behind.

She moped around the house a while longer, then drove into town to the police station, thinking Officer Huerta might have something for her to do. Huerta gave her the unpleasant task of cleaning out the supply closet. She was squatted on the floor, picking up tacks that had been spilled from a container, when Huerta poked her head around the doorjamb.

"Hey, girl, wanna see something?"

"What?" Anything was more interesting than the supply closet.

"Want to take a ride out to Promisedland with me and the fire chief? The Wheelers are building their bonfire structure, and the chief has to make sure it's up to code."

"Sure!" Kori jumped to her feet.

Fire Chief Bob Taylor was a friendly guy nearing retirement, with a handlebar mustache and a ring of gray curls circling his bald crown. He sat behind the wheel of his Goldhurst Fire Department car, with Officer Huerta riding shotgun and Kori in the backseat.

"I've been issuing these nutty people their fire permit every year since they've been here," he said. "Except for the first one, when they thought they could get away without one." He laughed. "When three fire trucks showed up the night of the big fire, they decided to go with the permit from then on."

"They got funny ideas, but they're harmless," said Huerta.

"I wouldn't say that," said Kori.

"Oh, really? While you were at Promisedland those times, did you see or hear of any illegal firearms?"

"No."

"Abusive punishments? People held against their will?"

"No, but they're brainwashed. It's a horrible life."

"It's their choice, Kori. What about drugs?"

Kori thought of Scorch's rotten teeth, but she had no hard evidence. She sighed. "Is drinking raw goat's milk against the law?"

Huerta lobbed her head over the seat. "It should be. What do you think they need such a big fire for?"

"I always thought they got naked and danced around it," said Chief Taylor.

"Naked people on private property isn't against the law either," said Huerta.

"What about human sacrifices?" asked Chief Taylor.

Huerta raised her forefinger. "Toasted naked people—definitely against the law."

Taylor and Huerta enjoyed the joke, while Kori privately shuttered. Pictures of people being burned at the stake in her middle school history book seemed all too real to laugh about. Still she was curious about what went on around Wheel of Fire's huge bonfire on Winter Solstice. She wished there was a way she could sneak in and spy on them, an unobserved outsider.

The gate was open at Promisedland and instead of parking near the ranch house, Chief Taylor turned down a dirt road leading to a fallow field, away from any trees or brush.

Wheel members were working inside a perfectly round pit about fifteen feet in diameter, which had been used for the fire in previous years. Promus wasn't in sight; neither were Flame, Ashe, or any of the other Inner Wheel members. When hard labor was to be done, it was up to Midwheel. Flicker was among the crew shoveling out the pit and smoothing it over with rakes. The Wheelers got down on their hands and knees and sifted the dirt for small pieces of debris. Every once in a while came a shout, "Here's another one," or "Sure glad I found this." Eventually Kori caught Flicker's eye, and she waved back.

Kori strode up to her. "Hey."

"Hey, you! What are you doing here?"

"Just watching. What are you taking out of the dirt?"

"Nails, staples. Metal in the fire is dangerous."

"Why?"

She smiled mysteriously, her eyes crinkling at the corners. "Come to Winter Solstice, and you'll see."

The workers began to layer the pit with black, shiny rocks. "What's that?" Kori asked.

"Coal."

"Oh. Duh." Kori felt dumb, but she had never actually seen coal.

The perimeter of the pit was then lined with sandbags. Workers gathered dry twigs, bark, and leaves to place in the center of the pit. A teepee was built over the tinder, small sticks and branches leaning against one another with gaps to allow oxygen to get to the kindling. The ends of the sticks were lashed at the top for stability. Chainsaws roared as logs were created to form the outside of the structure. Two logs were laid on opposite sides of the teepee, and then two more were laid perpendicular on top of the first two, log cabin style. When the construction was completed, it soared eighty feet high, a makeshift skyscraper waiting to scorch the Winter Solstice night.

Chief Taylor was satisfied with the work, signed the permit, and handed it to the Wheeler who was foreman of the structure. When he, Officer Huerta, and Kori got back into his car, he said, "One thing I'll say: they know how to build a fire."

"How do you think they light it?" Kori asked.

Huerta gave her a mock serious look over her shoulder. "I'm just guessing here, but I suppose they use a match."

Late in the afternoon, the next day, Kori was flopped on the sofa, bored to death, staring at her phone. "Ring, damn you, ring!"

Her cell remained inert, but she did hear ringing from the kitchen. For an instant, she couldn't think what it was. Then she remembered the landline! About the only calls they got on it were telephone solicitations. Usually it stopped after three rings, because some other sucker picked up, but this time Kori counted seven rings.

Only one person she knew would be that persistent. She dashed to the kitchen to answer it. "Hello?"

"Hey, Squirrel."

"Dad? Daddy? Where are you? Are you at the airport? Do you need me to come get you? Why didn't you tell us sooner when you were coming?"

"Hold on. I'm in New York—Fort Drum. I've got more training here before I return to Afghanistan with my brigade on an advising mission."

"Oh, but you do get some leave, right? You are still coming home."

Her dad sighed. That meant no. "I only have a couple of days, honey. Not worth flying all the way across the country. I got a buddy here in New York, though. She's taking me home to her mom's so you'll be happy to know your old man at least gets some Christmas dinner."

"What buddy? You didn't mention *her* in your letters."

"She's a private like me in my brigade. Private Tiffany Eggers."

Kori's heart thumped fiercely. "Does she have a husband?"

"Divorced. But she's got a little boy and girl, so it will be fun to be around some kids at Christmas."

"You have a son and a daughter, too."

"I never promised anything, Kori. It's just the way things worked out this Christmas. But hey, I haven't forgotten you. There's a big check in the mail coming your way. You can pick out whatever you like, or just squirrel it away like you usually do. I hope I'm not spoiling you."

"I don't want money. I want you, Daddy! Come home. Please!"

"Merry Christmas, Kori," he said forlornly.

"Nothing merry about it," she snapped.

"I'll call you back when you're in a better mood."

"Would you like to speak to Mom?"

"I gotta go. Just tell her hi."

Her dad hung up before she could say her mom wasn't there, gone off on a tryst with douchebag Vaughn. No one was there. Kori was utterly alone. Tears flowed down her cheeks. She squeezed her eyes shut, letting the raw disappointment sink into her bones like the bitter cold. She had been so sure her dad was coming home, insisting on it to her mom and Jared. They were right: her dad didn't give a shit about them. Private Tiffany Eggers—who the fuck? Jared had tried to warn her.

Kori's cell phone dinged to announce an incoming text, probably from her mom or Luke. It was from an unknown caller:

"Invitation still stands. It's not too late to see the biggest fire of your life. Say you'll be here."

"Flicker! I'll be there."

Chapter Fifteen

Dusk arrived early on the shortest day of the year. A long stream of cars crept along the shoulder of Blue Ridge Road, waiting for entrance into Promisedland. Each visitor was carefully checked, and nonmembers were turned away. Kori expected she'd have some explaining to do, but a Wheeler she'd never met waved her through with a grin as if he recognized her.

Kori parked her truck with the other vehicles in the dirt lot near the ranch house. Flicker ran out to greet her with a hug. Kori had taught her the trick of curling her hair with strips of rags, and it rippled in ringlets over a fluffy white sweater she had never seen before.

"You look gorgeous!"

"Really?" Flicker's eyes shone with the compliment. "I took your advice and found some girl clothes. Do you think Promus will notice?"

"He'd have to be blind not to!" Kori started to walk again, but Flicker caught her shoulder.

"I mean would he be attracted…if I knocked on his door tonight?"

Kori stared back at her. She had a gut feeling that Promus would *not* accept Flicker.

"Forget it."

"No, Flicker! It's just that I don't know his tastes. You could try."

"I couldn't *try.* It would have to be a sure thing, or I'd die of shame." She stared in the distance a moment, and then smiled at Kori. "Ah, come on, let's eat!"

This was definitely not a "raw food" night. The buffet table was loaded with hams, turkeys, slabs of beef, and all the trimmings. Flicker and Kori piled their plates high and dug in enthusiastically.

Roberta and Rayann were seated across from them. Rayann looked old and feeble, her dowager hump more pronounced as she hunched over her meal. “The fire is just too big,” she muttered. “I worry that it’s going to rage out of control one of these years.”

Roberta wasn’t in a festive mood either. “I just don’t like staying up so late. This old girl would rather take a sleeping pill, go to bed, and forget the whole thing.”

Rayann touched her sister’s shoulder with a concerned look. “I thought you weren’t taking your sleeping pills anymore.”

“Don’t worry, dear. Usually not. But it’s going to be *loud* tonight.”

Kori scanned the servers, who were replenishing drinks and collecting empty plates. “I haven’t seen Ember tonight. Where is she?”

“Probably resting,” Flicker commented, exchanging a concerned look with Roberta.

“Is her cough any better?” Kori asked.

“Oh, yes,” said Flicker. “Real Father prays over her every day.”

A lot of good that does. Kori scarfed down a generous piece of pumpkin pie. By then the crowd was thinning out. “Oh, have we missed the lighting of the fire?”

Flicker shook her head, her upper lip dotted with whipped cream. “Oh, no. That won’t happen until everyone’s outside, but we better get going.” She looked longingly at the stack of sugar cookies still on her plate.

“Take them to go, sweetie.” Roberta wrapped them in a paper napkin for her.

“Thanks.” Flicker lightly kissed her rosy, wrinkled cheek. “Don’t sneak off upstairs now.”

“We’ll be along,” answered Roberta. “You girls go ahead.”

In the foyer Kori and Flicker put on jackets, scarves, earmuffs, and gloves. Outside, they felt their way along the dirt path leading to the bonfire site, relying on the people ahead of them as guides. Someone stumbled and swore, while Wheelers around him snickered and whispered, “Be careful!” No flashlights or other illumination was allowed, Flicker explained, because it would detract from the dramatic lighting of the fire.

When they reached the clearing, the bonfire structure stood like a black tower against the clear, starry night. People had gathered in a single circle, Outer and Midwheel members mingling, because the perimeter of the bonfire pit was so large. An opening of the circle was cordoned off with stakes, probably reserved for Promus and the twelve Inner Wheel members when they made their entrance.

Flicker crowded in next to the right stake, joining six other Wheel women, who wore tacky-looking evening gowns and too much makeup like little girls playing dress-up. "Excuse us," said Flicker. "We're supposed to be here, too."

A woman with streaks of dark rouge along her cheekbones like war paint looked them up and down. "Since when did you become a Holy Vessel, Flicker?"

"I didn't, Glimmer, but Ashe told us to stand here. That makes me a candidate, too."

Glimmer scooted over a few inches, but didn't look that happy about it.

"Candidate for what?" Kori asked Flicker.

She cupped her mouth to whisper in her ear. "Remember when Real Father said I'd be rewarded? I think this is it! I'm getting a special honor."

"What?" Kori asked.

Flicker grinned mischievously "Shh! You'll see."

They waited over an hour, stomping their numb feet, the Holy Vessels rubbing their goose bumps and shivering. Other Wheelers muttered speculations, their milky breath floating in the chilly air. Finally, in the distance, came the faint sounds of the Inner Wheel procession, accompanied by drums, gongs, and finger cymbals. As its members drew closer, Kori could make out the silhouettes of their capes, sweeping the ground. Inner Wheelers stopped before the left stake, but didn't fill in the circle. Promus, in his bejeweled cape, held another cape before him. The gongs and finger cymbals were silenced, but the drumming continued in slow, loud, methodical pulses, like the beating of a monster's heart.

Promus stepped behind Kori and placed the cape over her shoulders, then fastened the clasp beneath her chin. Ashe handed her the automatic torch he always carried into services. Cheers, whistling, hoots, and laughter erupted from the Wheel. It took Kori a moment to realize Promus was applying pressure between her shoulder blades. As he spun her around, she glimpsed Flicker's sullen eyes glaring at her. Glimmer's fists were clenched as she and the other Holy Vessels scowled. Kori's heart raced. Why had Promus singled her out when it was obvious these other women expected to be chosen? Now he was pushing her down a dark trail in the opposite direction of the ranch house.

Murmurs rose from the waiting crowd, "What now?"

"Where are they going?"

"We've waited long enough!"

"Promus! Always has to make such a big production out of this!"

"Hot little fire starter. Maybe he's got to have her first."

"That's Real Father, a man of ravenous appetites."

Promus ignored the comments as he pressed Kori on. She tried to look back at him, but he grasped the back of her head and twisted, forcing her to look ahead.

"Wait your step," he said gently.

"Wh-where are we going?"

"You'll see."

Kori's blood pounded in her ears. She wished Officer Huerta hadn't made that joke about human sacrifices. She stopped so abruptly Promus bumped into her.

"I don't want to do this. I'm afraid."

"Of me, General of God's army in the Armageddon? You'd better fear Satan instead." He nudged her on, but she resisted.

"Tell me what we're doing."

"We're on a mission. Trust me, sweetheart, you'll like it."

"Like *what*?" She didn't like the sound of "sweetheart." If he forced himself on her, she would fight and scream; she didn't care what the others thought of her.

"Patience, my daughter. You'll see."

They were steadily climbing, and when they reached the summit of a low bluff, Promus said, "This is the place." They had not traveled far, only about fifty feet from the bonfire structure, but it had seemed much longer in the dark on the winding trail.

Promus leaned over some brush and extracted a duffle bag and a shotgun.

"What's that for?" Kori asked, trying to keep her voice steady. She tightened her grip on the heavy torch she carried, the only weapon she held against him. If he pointed the shotgun at her, she would try to bat it out of his hands, hit him over the head, and run.

"You're going to light my fire." He wrenched the torch from her hands and flung it over the cliff. "We won't be needing this piece of shit."

Kori watched it cartwheel down the incline until it disappeared in the darkness. *Fire starter.* It was the honor Flicker and the Holy Vessels were hoping for. Kori wasn't even a member of his club. "Why me?"

"I have prayed long and hard about this, my daughter. God told me to test you."

"God talked to you?"

"Through the angel, always through Michael."

Kori thought of the Bible story about Abraham, whom God tested by commanding him to kill his son, Isaac. "Test me for what?"

He chuckled. "I want to see if you're as good a shot as I think you are."

"It's unlikely a shell fired from this range would ignite a fire even if you've got some flint and lighter fluid imbedded in the tinder. Besides, there's people down there!"

"Do you think I'd let you shoot my own people?"

"The buckshot will spray."

He nodded toward the shotgun. "My dear girl, this isn't loaded with shot."

"What then?"

From the duffle bag, he extracted some high tech goggles and slipped them over her head.

"Cool!" They were not only equipped with infrared night vision but also had a telescopic lens. Down below, each person shimmered in dazzling reds, yellows, and purples. Now it was apparent why no one stood between the two stakes. It was the target. Promus handed her the shotgun. She shouldered it and took aim. It was a pretty easy shot, but it was also possible that she could hit someone. She lowered the gun. "I can't. My arm is shaking."

"I'll help you." Promus tossed aside the capes they wore and stood behind her, his whole body pressed against hers, his low even breath warming her ear, his heartbeat pulsing against her back. He slowly raised her arm with his palm to take aim. "By the way," he whispered, "you only get one shot."

What did she feel at that instant? *Power.* Kori squeezed the trigger. A rocket of fire arced into the air. Sparks glowed within the structure, and in moments, flames leaped out the top. Cheers and applause erupted from the gathering. Kori slowly eased the shotgun off her shoulder. "Wow! Was that a flare?"

"Dragon's Breath."

"Cool name. Is it legal?"

When Promus didn't answer, Kori turned to look at him. Sweat poured in rivulets down his temples, his labored breathing whistled through his clenched, square teeth, and his eyes glistened brightly. The face of a madman. She had been ridiculous to think he might attack her. She may as well not have been there. Promus was gazing at the glowing fire as if it were the love of his life.

Kori didn't remember the walk back. Abruptly she was beside the fire, the cape, which she now discovered was scarlet in color, again circling her shoulders. Promus raised his arms and rested his hands on her head, announcing in a loud, bellowing voice, "Now you are one of us. You are Kori Lawton no more. I christen you Kindle."

The Wheel of Fire members rushed her, grasping her hands, hugging her, congratulating her as this year's fire starter. She looked into their elated faces, her protests lodged in her throat. She spotted Flicker, standing several paces back from the circle, in light and shadow, her arms crossed and her eyes cast away from the festivities. Kori walked up to her and touched her elbow.

Flicker glared at her, her eyes blazing knots of reflected fire. "It's not fair! I've been in the Wheel for eighteen months! I've done everything Promus has asked me! Begging, recruiting, groveling! Pressing kidnapping charges against my own parents! For a reward. Where's my reward? And you—you're not even one of us! You don't even *believe!* Why do *you* get to be fire starter?"

"I don't know." She thought about Promus telling her it was God's wish. "I don't understand any of this."

"Kindle!" someone yelled.

"Fire starter Kindle, come!"

"Kindle, we're waiting for you to begin."

Flicker turned her head away. "Go on! Your fan club is calling you."

Kori hadn't recognized the name. She returned to the circle and found Roberta and Rayann. "Flicker is really upset. Could you guys go talk to her?"

The elderly sisters went to Flicker, spoke to her in hushed voices, then returned to the ring on either side of her, encircling her shoulders. Everyone held hands around the fire.

Promus began the litany. "Come, holy spirit of Michael the Archangel."

"Come, holy spirit of Michael the Archangel," replied his people.

"Come, spirit of Michael."

"Come, spirit of Michael."

In her mind, Kori was back up on the hill in the darkness, aiming the shotgun at the black structure, her finger twitching on the trigger. It had been the most terrifying and exciting moment of her life. She *knew* she could do what Promus had asked of her. She was the chosen one.

The pulse traveled rapidly around the Wheel of over a hundred people. Like in previous services, Kori anticipated the arrival of the pulse each time it passed through her. She had missed this. She craved this. She was thrilled to be a part of this living pulse, to feel it course through her again and again.

Then it happened: Kori was engulfed by the spirit.

A rush of power entered her through the left side of her head and bore through her body like a whirling cyclone. A warm glow filled her being as if the fire before her had leaped into her soul. All her worries and disappointment, pain and anger, were released from her being. She felt such rapture that she thought she'd fly.

When had her feet begun moving? Still facing the fire, her hands clasped with the other Wheel members, she was sidestepping to the right, dancing around and around the fire. Sweat dripping from her face, she wanted to throw off the heavy cape and her jacket, but she could not bear to break the bonds of the Wheel.

The blazing structure shifted and tumbled. The flames licked the air only fifteen feet above the ground, then ten, then it was eye level, then all that remained was a bed of glimmering coals. The people unclasped their hands, laughing and hooting. The instruments were taken up and played. Icy sparkling water was served in silver goblets. Some of the members stripped down to shorts and tank tops in the cold winter air. The bravest of them removed their shoes and socks.

Promus faced the pit of glowing coals. The drum beat pulsed again, deep and slow. He stepped onto the fire, one bare foot and then the other, strolling gingerly, but leisurely across the diameter, his white square teeth gleaming in a proud leer. When he reached the other side, a roar of appreciation rose up from the crowd, along with whistles and applause. Promus bowed deeply, almost comically, as a tightrope walker completing a performance.

Flame followed next on her fire walk, waving her arms, swinging her hips seductively, as she crossed the burning pit. Ashe came next, then Stix. The Wheelers shouted out names, coaxing or daring their friends to take the challenge. Some Wheelers accepted it, but others shook their heads, grinning sheepishly.

"Haven't you enough faith?" the Wheelers goaded. "Don't you believe the spirit of Michael will protect your flesh from burning?"

Flame sat on the ground, wiping the ash from her soles to replace her socks and boots. Kori crouched next to her and peered at her feet.

"Looking for burns?"

"Kinda," Kori admitted. "How is it possible?"

"It's not hard if you stay in control. You must focus your mind on the fact that the coals cannot burn you if you don't allow them to. The worst thing is to panic and run."

"Wouldn't running decrease the time of contact with the hot coals?"

"It causes the feet to bear down on the heat. That's what causes burns."

"I'd chicken out."

"Then don't try it," Flame smiled at her with her eyes. For the first time, Flame expressed affection toward her. Kori was the chosen. Even Flame would have to accept her now.

As Kori stood, the chants rose up, "Kindle! Kindle! Kindle!"

She shook her head, smiling apologetically.

"Kindle! Kindle! Kindle!" On and on they shouted her fire name in time to the pounding drums.

"Ah, leave her alone," said Ashe. "She's not ready."

"The spirit is with me!" exclaimed Flicker. Hopping on one foot then the other, she tore off her shoes and socks and threw them in all directions.

She stood before the fire pit, staring at the coals and snorting like a bull about to charge.

Promus strode up behind her and gripped her shoulders. "This is not a good idea, my timid daughter."

Flicker shook off his hands. In her narrowed eyes Kori saw her anger mixed with a desperate determination. Flicker placed one bare, white foot onto the coals and then the other. Her first few steps were sure and steady, in synch with the tempo of the drum. She winced, quickened her pace. A flash of horror twisted her countenance. Then, with a mournful, wailing scream, she sprinted across of the searing coals. She threw herself into the dirt on her back, moaning and clutching her feet, writhing in pain. No one approached to soothe her.

Kori should rush to her friend's aid, but frankly she didn't feel like it. Promus had warned Flicker: she was weak in spirit. Kori sat down to unlace her shoes. Did she want to show up Flicker? Honestly, no. She wanted to perform the fire walk simply because she could. She was the chosen.

What does it take to walk across burning coals? Kori found out that night. It was a matter of placing one foot in front of the other with the firm belief that she felt nothing. When she reached the other side, the cheers sounded muffled in her ears. She had not performed for an audience; she had acted on faith. She gazed across the valley at the thin ribbon of light outlining distant Blue Ridge Mountain, the dawn of a new day, the beginning of her new life as a believer. "Praise God," she whispered to herself. "Praise Michael."

Winter Solstice was over. Many townsfolk had already driven away; some residents of Promisedland had gone to bed. Other Wheelers were gathering their outer garments, heading toward the ranch house, where a huge breakfast would be served. Kori wasn't hungry, and she no longer wanted to be with people. She stepped toward her truck, without bidding a single person good-bye, lost inside herself, harboring the spirit of Michael.

Chapter Sixteen

In the early morning gray, Kori walked into her empty house. Her mom and Vaughn wouldn't be home until late afternoon. Her dad wasn't coming home at all. Not that it mattered, not anymore. She got into her pajamas and lay in bed, mulling over the events of the night. Launching the Dragon's Breath into the waiting dark structure was scary and thrilling at once. She wanted to do it again and again. She wondered if she would ever have another chance. Probably not. Probably there would be a different fire starter next year. Now she understood Flicker's jealousy and resentment toward her. Poor Flicker! Her poor feet!

She couldn't get back that warm glow of the spirit of Michael within her, but just thinking about it made her feel calm and good. Her life had made a sudden, startling turn, but now she was on the path toward everlasting life with her Heavenly Father. She had no qualms that she had made the right choice. It wasn't her choice, really; God had chosen her. She drifted off, and when she awoke it was nearly noon.

Kori rolled over, but she couldn't get back to sleep. She got up, dressed, ate, and tried to read, but her mind wandered. Soon she was driving into town. She had to confide in somebody, and since neither her mom nor Luke was around, it had to be Officer Huerta.

When Kori walked into her office, Huerta peered over the half-glasses she wore when she was working at her computer. "You're not on the schedule."

Kori shoved her hands into her jean pockets and sauntered in. "I know. I just thought you might need me for something."

"There's always the dog kennels. I didn't get around to cleaning them yesterday with all that hoopla going on at the Wheel compound. We had to keep patrolling the place making sure those loonies didn't torch the whole valley."

Kori winced at the term. "It was a controlled bonfire. I…I was there."

Huerta slipped off her glasses. "How'd you get in?"

"Flicker invited me."

"Well, well! I've always wanted to know—what's it like?"

Kori shrugged. "Big. Hot."

"Did you all get naked?"

"It's a religious ceremony! We prayed for the spirit of St. Michael to come to us. And, ma'am, it happened to me!" Kori announced forcefully.

Huerta cocked her head, her brow furrowed. "Say what?"

"The spirit entered me like–*wham!*–an explosion inside me. It was the most awesome thing I ever felt."

Officer Huerta wrinkled her nose. "Did they give you something to eat or drink?"

"Drugs? No. It was real." Huerta was looking at Kori so strangely, she felt compelled to explain further. "You believe in Jesus and the Resurrection, right? And the Second Coming and Armageddon, just like Wheel of Fire."

"Armageddon—I don't know about. I prefer Judgment Day. We're all gonna get judged by God in the end. I believe that."

Kori pulled up a chair close to her desk. "What does faith feel like to you?"

"Not like *wham.* No fire and explosions. Hmm…" Huerta tipped her chin to the ceiling, thinking. "It's a peaceful feeling. That I'm not alone out there on patrol." She swept her arm around her cluttered office. "That there's something more after this." She was quiet for a long time. Too long. Kori shifted in her chair. Finally Huerta asked, "So you're a member of the club now?"

Kori cheeks flushed hotly. "Yes."

"A follower of Promus?"

She had to admit it to someone. She nodded slowly.

"Oh, Kori, how did you let this happen? Are you moving into the compound?"

"It's not a compound; it's a community! You know I wouldn't leave my mom, and I'm going away to college next year."

"Not if Promus doesn't want you to. Not if he wants to keep you at his beck and call."

Since middle school, Kori had dreamed of earning a degree in criminology. What if Promus didn't allow her to go to college? He would have to! He would have to understand how important it was to her. "He's sent other Wheelers to college. I know of several. Flame has an accounting degree; Ashe is a lawyer."

"Yeah, to keep ole Promus out of jail."

"You think it's criminal that the Wheel's beliefs are different from other churches?"

Huerta held up both palms. "Don't get defensive, girl. I just wonder where Promus gets all the funds to support sixty-some people, build a small village, and live a life of luxury."

"Donations!"

"Oh, I know about all that, but something doesn't quite add up. And Dower left Wyoming for a reason—a reason that hasn't come to light."

"His intolerant neighbors set fire to his property!"

"Maybe," Huerta said thoughtfully. "He never was able to collect the insurance because he never could prove he didn't set the fire himself."

"What? That's crazy!"

"For a long time we've suspected Promus *is* crazy." Her eyes widened in emphasis. "Crazy about fire."

Kori's feet began to itch. She wriggled them in her shoes, but that didn't help. She excused herself to use the restroom. As soon as she locked the door, she pulled off her shoes and socks and inspected her soles. They were lobster red, like she had fallen asleep on her stomach on the beach. Then she remembered: she had walked on fire.

When Kori got home, she saw Luke's truck parked in her driveway. Even though he had been gone nearly a week, she wasn't that excited to see him. She wondered why he hadn't texted first, and then she remembered her phone was still off from the previous night. When she slid out of her truck, he rushed to her and scooped her up in a big hug.

Kori stiffened in his embrace. When he kissed her, she flinched.

He pulled away from her, holding her at arm's length. "What's the matter?"

"Nothing. I'm just tired."

"No, there's something. You've changed. You look completely different. You're looking at me like I'm a stranger."

Her eyes slid away from his.

"Tell me, Kori. Is there someone else?"

"No! I mean…yes, but not the way you think."

His arms flopped to his sides, but he was silent, waiting for her to go on.

"Flicker invited me to the Winter Solstice Celebration and—"

Luke shoved her backward, glaring at her. "Promus!" He spit the word like something vile. "He got to you, didn't he? I knew he would with you hanging around those Wheelers! That shithead got my mom, and now he's got my girl!"

"Don't call him that! You don't even know him. You don't understand."

"I understand my mom needs medical attention, and he's too cheap to pay for it. I'll bet standing outside in the cold all night didn't help her."

"Luke, she wasn't out by the fire. I didn't see her all night! I'll check on her the next time I go to Promisedland."

"You told me there wasn't going to be a next time, and now you're in!" He spun around and stomped toward his truck.

"Luke! Wait! Don't be mad. We can still be…" Kori stopped. She didn't really know what they could be now. Everything in her life was changed, including her feelings for Luke. Now she looked on him not as a boyfriend, not a friend. Rather, a soul to save.

Luke leaped into his truck, slammed the door, and roared off.

Chapter Seventeen

It was so lonely opening presents Christmas morning with just her mom and herself that Kori could hardly stand to go through the motions. Why did everybody buy a bunch of crap for each other at Christmas, anyway? What did it have to do with Jesus's birth or Second Coming? It was stupid and meaningless. With three wrapped gifts still in her pile on the sofa, Kori got up and gazed out the front window toward Promisedland, filled with the people who understood her and the Real Father who loved her. She pretended to think of her own dad. "I still can't believe Daddy isn't here for Christmas."

"Too bad, Kori. We can't always get what we want." Cindy lit a cigarette.

"Mom, please. Not in the house."

"It's my house." When Kori had told her mom she had joined Wheel of Fire, Cindy took up smoking again, seven years after she quit.

"Smoking is bad from you." Kori tried to hug her mom, but Cindy pushed her away.

"You're lost to me," she said. "Just like your brother and your dad."

That afternoon, in the visitors' room at Corcoran Prison, Cindy turned on Kori with arched eyebrows. "Tell your brother what you've been up to."

Judging by Jared's smirk, Cindy had already clued him in. "Well, 'lil sis, if you need a new father figure, you sure as hell can do better than Promus."

"That's not what it's about!" Kori said heatedly.

"Hell, I need a cigarette," said Cindy, bolting from her chair.

"Save one for me," Jared called after her. He grinned his shit-eating grin at Kori. "Got to admit it's ironic."

"Right. She leads the campaign in getting you to quit. Now look at her."

"I'm not talking about smoking. Daddy—Real Father. Sick."

"You don't know anything about it!"

"I'm just sayin' there might be a connection."

"How could you possibly understand, Jared? You don't believe in anything!"

"Hey, I'm Christian!"

Kori studied Jared's face, expecting a sardonic leer that didn't come. "You are?"

He nodded solemnly. "Jesus forgives, right? If I didn't believe in second chances, I might as well give up here and now. So what do you believe, 'lil sis? Promus is god?"

"No!" Kori heaved, tears welling up. "I don't know about him, Jared. He scares me." She pressed her forefinger to her breast. "I started that bonfire." In a hoarse whisper, she described the hike up the dark path, aiming down at the structure, and firing the Dragon's Breath.

"Fucking awesome!" shouted Jared, his face aglow. "I've heard of Dragon's Breath, but I've never seen it. You realize you could've killed some folks."

"That's just it!" Kori nearly hissed. "I *didn't* realize it, when it was the rational thing to do. With Promus at my back, it was like he was controlling me. Another time—the first time—I was with him, I fired a rifle with no intention of doing it. It's like he *made* me do it, and I don't know how!"

"Don't be dumb, Kori. You're always hassling me for doing time for Ciclón, well, don't you take the fall for Real Dad."

"Villadez is a criminal. Promus is a man of God!"

"Don't be too sure. I hear things."

"Vicious rumors, spread by Promus's enemies!" Kori swiped at her eyes, ashamed that she had expressed doubts about Real Father to her brother.

Jared tipped back on two legs of his chair. "Promus likes two things: controlling people and setting fires."

"You've got no proof!"

"You're right, I don't." He let the front of his chair crash down on the linoleum, inches from her right big toe. "I'm just saying watch yourself. Decide here and now: no one can make you do what you don't want to do, not even Promus."

When Kori returned to school after New Year's, she began to live a double life: Wheel of Fire member and regular teen girl. She and Luke continued to hang out and lift weights together. Sometimes she went over to his house to help him with his chores or read and play with the kids. Kori and Luke looked like a couple, but the delicious sessions of kissing and touching and gazing into each other's eyes were over. An invisible wedge drove them apart, and they seemed to have an unspoken agreement not to talk about it. The only thing that would make things right between them was if Luke joined the Wheel, but she didn't dare to hope for it.

Kori continued as an Explorer for the Goldhurst Police Department, joining Officer Huerta on ride-alongs, but she did less of it. Her dream of becoming a detective was fading. She spent as much time as possible participating in Wheel activities: food gathering, fund raising, and attending two or three church services a week. She felt joy in those services, but never again the explosive power of the spirit of Michael alighting in her soul at Winter Solstice.

Kori saw a lot of Promus at the various activities and services. He didn't single her out or demand her to do anything special. She thought of Jared's cautionary words, but evidently there was no cause for concern. Occasionally Promus stroked her hair or rested his palm on the small of her back, but that was all the attention he gave her. That didn't stop her from thinking about his body pressed against her back just before she shot the Dragon's Breath to ignite the fire. She had erotic dreams about him, and she couldn't help wondering if eventually she'd be compelled to knock on his door, his answering, and her opening herself to him.

Kori suffered gut-wrenching guilt over her serves-her-right attitude toward Flicker when she had burned her feet on the hot coals. She took on the responsibility of changing her dressing and bandages, and in a couple of weeks Flicker was able to walk again in light, mincing steps. Her feet would probably never completely heal without plastic surgery, an expense Promus wouldn't allow. To cheer her up, Kori smuggled in unauthorized junk food–homemade chocolate chip cookies, sweet and sour pork, and french fries. Flicker gobbled these treats greedily, and Kori took pleasure in watching her enjoy them. None of the girls at school and at Explorers interested her. Who else but Flicker could possibly understand her? They found a way to be together during every Wheel activity, occasionally breaking the rules by straying from their designated "Four Horsemen" for some private girl talk.

Since she no longer had to shun her family, Flicker talked openly about her life before the Wheel. Once when they were weeding the vegetable garden, Kori noticed Flicker pause to gaze longingly after Promus crossing the property on horseback. "Doesn't Real Father look fine on his black stallion?"

"Ah, he's okay for a cult leader."

"Don't call him that!"

Kori laughed. "I've got it figured out why you're attracted to older men. It's because your high school boyfriend hurt you."

"Tristan? That asshole." She threw a dirt clod at Kori's shoe.

She dodged it, laughing. "How's Ember today?"

"Better."

That's what Flicker always said, but Kori wanted proof. Stix had taken over Ember's role as Lead Gatherer, since she was too weak to manage it. "As soon as we get done here, let's go visit her," suggested Kori.

"Oh, we shouldn't disturb her. She's resting."

Kori straightened, then arched her back in a stretch. "I want to see her!"

Flicker tugged against an especially large, stubborn weed, her hair flopping over her face. "She's not accepting visitors."

"Is she dead?" Kori asked flatly.

"Who—Ember?" Flicker asked absently. "No."

"That's it, isn't it? She died, and Ashe stuffed her body somewhere." Kori cupped her palm over her brow and looked across the field. "Let's see, now. Any shallow graves out there?"

"God damn it, Kori. Stop!"

"Ha! Made you swear."

"I'll show you where she is. Just shut up, will you?"

They finished their weeding, then washed the crusted dirt off their hands, using the garden hose. Flicker led Kori through the back door of the ranch house. They went up the stairs and down the hall of the women's dormitory. Flicker opened the door of a dark bedroom. It contained three bunk beds, but held only one occupant, with tangled, gray-streaked black hair sticking out of a sleeping bag. Kori took a step into the room, and Flicker grasped her forearm to stop her.

"She's asleep!"

From where Kori was standing, she couldn't be sure the person was actually Ember. She shook loose of Flicker, and was tiptoeing toward the bed when Ashe's voice boomed behind them. "There you are! What are the two of you doing alone?"

"I wanted to see Ember," Kori whispered.

"Can't you see she needs her rest?" scolded Ashe. "You're wanted in the Inner Wheel meeting room."

"I am?" Flicker said excitedly.

"Not you. Kindle."

Flicker bowed her head. Kori squeezed her hand sympathetically, and then followed Ashe downstairs to the Inner Wheel's den. Gathered around the table were Promus, Flame, Scorch, and Match. Match was a skinhead who had even shaved his eyebrows, which made him look surprised and stupid. He had the Wheel of Fire logo—a crucifix on fire inside a circle—tattooed on the back of his skull. Kori remembered that Flicker had told her that Flame tried to keep Scorch and Match separated. Promus approached Ashe and Kori and shut the door behind them. He draped his arm over her shoulders and steered her to an empty chair next to his. Kori felt uneasy. She wished Flicker were with her for moral support.

Flame looked up at Promus from the spreadsheet open on her laptop. "What's she doing here?"

"She's our fire starter!" Promus exclaimed.

Flame flicked her hair over her shoulder in annoyance. "Winter Solstice was a month ago."

"We have a mission," Promus announced.

Flame narrowed her eyes at him. "What sort of mission?"

Promus leered at his wife. "Protecting God's earth." He placed under an Elmo document camera a photograph of a picturesque mountainside overlooking Lake Tahoe. "We're going to prevent this from becoming this." He replaced the photo with a drawing of the same scene covered with a massive hotel and casino complex. "Construction has already begun, but we can stop it."

"How do you propose we do that?" Flame asked, an edge to her tone that alarmed Kori. For a long moment, Promus and Flame were locked in a hostile staring match.

"The usual way," Promus said matter-of-factly.

"No, you don't, Vince! You promised you put an end to that the last time."

"I've been commissioned by the Michael the Archangel to protect God's earth."

"I'll have no part of this." Flame bolted from the room with such fury that her chair fell back onto the title with an echoing clatter. Ashe cast his eyes after her, but maintained his position at the table. Promus shrugged as if to say he didn't need Flame's approval.

"We need your help with this, Kindle," he stated. "Are you in?"

Jared's words reverberated in her head: *Watch yourself, don't be dumb.* Her heart raced and her throat felt dry. "What…what do I have to do?"

"Join us." He tapped the drawing. "Put a little pressure on these developers."

"You mean like a kind of protest?"

Scorch snickered, exposing the stumps of his ruined teeth. Match rubbed his hands together and leered.

"Yes," said Promus, also enjoying the private joke. "You might say it's like a protest."

Kori didn't want any part of a scheme that Scorch and Match would enjoy. "I've got school," she said warily.

"Can't you miss a day or two for your Real Father?"

"Who else is coming?"

Promus waved his hand toward Match and Scorch.

"I don't want to be the only girl! Can Flicker come?"

"She'll screw things up," said Scorch. "She can't even walk straight."

Match and Promus laughed.

"That's mean!" Kori turned on Promus. "She's totally devoted to you, and you treat her like crap."

Promus held up his palm. "Peace, my daughter. Flicker has been asking for more responsibility. This could be a good test for her. If you agree to the mission, she can come along."

"I want something else," Kori said.

Promus reared back. "You dare to bargain with me?" He seemed more amused than annoyed.

"I want Ember to see a doctor."

Promus nodded, thoughtfully. "I was considering that myself." He patted her head. "You and I think alike, Kindle. If you perform well on the mission, when we return, you can take Ember to the doctor yourself."

"I can? Oh, great! I'm all in."

The sound of running footsteps and loud exclamations erupted from the hall.

"What the hell?" asked Promus, half rising.

Ashe, who was closest to the door, flung it open. About a dozen residents were clamoring past them. Promus went to see what the commotion was, and everyone in the room followed him, through the great room, and out to the front yard. Wheelers were gathered in a circle and in its center was Stix, his arms raised, his horned-rimmed glasses reflecting the sun, his face aglow.

"I have seen the angel!" he exclaimed. "Rejoice! I have seen Michael the Archangel!"

Promus stomped his way through the gathering to confront Stix. He was about a foot shorter than the newly self-proclaimed prophet, and he had to crane his neck to meet Stix's beatific gaze. "You have *not* seen the angel!" he roared, giving Stix's chest a menacing thump. "Only I can see the angel!"

Flame sauntered toward the two men, her orange hair flickering like fire behind her, her lips pursed in a simper. "We've witnessed it ourselves, Promus. We saw Stix out here in the yard speaking to the angel. It seems Stix can see the angel just as well as you can!"

"Foolish woman!" Promus raised a threatening palm against her. "Can't you tell when someone is experiencing a true vision and when someone is staging a hoax?" Promus turned his back on Stix and with sweeping arms began herding his people inside the house. "Come with me, my sons and daughters, back to what you were doing. Ignore this false prophet and his senseless ravings."

The Wheelers cooperated, but reluctantly, gazing back at Stix, whose countenance still bore a saintly expression.

"If Stix claims he saw the angel, it must be true," Roberta muttered to her sister.

Rayann nodded. "Certainly he is an honest man, but I can see it's going to take Promus some getting used to."

Chapter Eighteen

If Kori straight up told her mom that she was going away for three days with Promus and some other Wheelers, her mom would put her foot down. Kori could say she was going somewhere with friends from school, but she didn't want to lie. She decided she would take the chicken way out and leave a note under the saltshaker before sneaking out of the house early Saturday morning.

Friday, just before the lunch bell, Kori got a pass from the office, stating that her brother was there to take her to a doctor's appointment. Kori knew it couldn't be Jared, and wondered which Wheeler came for her, probably to finalize plans for the mission. In the school office, Kori found Match, wearing a baseball cap to cover his shaved head and the Wheel of Fire tat on the back of his skull. He led Kori out to an old blue sedan that she had never seen before, with Promus in the passenger's seat and Scorch and Flicker in the backseat. Match opened the trunk and asked Kori for her backpack, which he added to suitcases, sleeping bags, a cooler, and other supplies they would need on the mission the following day. Kori got in the backseat and Match got behind the wheel.

"Surprise!" said Flicker, giving her a hug.

"Shut up!" Promus ordered. He pointed to Flicker over the seat. "You do not have permission to speak."

The atmosphere in the car grew tense. Match drove onto Highway 99, heading north. They passed Tulare, Visalia, and were coming into Fresno.

"Where are we going?" Kori asked, trying to force down the panic in her voice.

"We're on the mission!" Flicker said excitedly.

Promus made a motion as if to backhand her. "Silence!"

"I'm not packed!" Kori said. "I thought we were going tomorrow."

"We've got everything you need," Promus said with a chuckle, then added, "Haven't we, boys?"

"I do," said Scorch. "What about you, Travis?"

"Me, too, Joe."

Were these the two ex-Ghoul members Jared had told her about? "Hey, do you guys know my brother?" Kori asked Scorch.

"We are your brothers," he replied, sharing a leering grin with Match in the rearview mirror.

East of Sacramento, the travelers stopped for gas and a bathroom break. Promus allowed Flicker and Kori to go to the women's room, one at a time so they couldn't speak to each other. While Flicker was in the restroom, Kori asked for her backpack to get her phone out.

"You don't need your phone," said Promus.

"My mom doesn't know where I am!"

"Good."

"Not good. She'll worry."

"It can't be helped, Kindle sweetheart," said Promus. "This is a secret mission. No one can know our whereabouts, not even your mom."

"Why is it secret?" Kori asked. "This is the first I've heard of any secret." Promus didn't answer. Her pounding heart told her something was very wrong. She never should have agreed to this.

Everyone got back in the car, and they drove on to Lake Tahoe. Near the Nevada state line, they avoided the towering hotel-casinos and turned into one of the shabby motels on Pioneer Trail. While Match went in the office to register, Scorch opened the trunk, unloaded the supplies, and handed Kori her backpack. She took out her phone to check for messages and found it smashed to pieces.

"Ah, too bad," said Scorch with his snaggletooth grin. "How could that have happened?"

The five Wheelers crowded into a single room with two queen-sized beds. It smelled of stale cigarette smoke; the carpet was threadbare and stained. Match lit a dish of fire on the nightstand between the two beds. Scorch unpacked fruit, nuts, and water for dinner. Flicker and Kori were to share one of the beds, and Promus got the other one. Match and Scorch had to sleep on the floor in sleeping bags. "Just like home," commented Scorch.

Kori was sitting on the edge of her assigned bed, waiting her turn to use the sink, when Promus handed her a toothbrush, still in its package.

"Please let me call my mom," she pleaded. "Just to let her know I'm okay."

"Ah, she's probably out carousing with lover boy and hasn't given you a thought."

It was true that Vaughn often met Cindy in town after she got off work on Fridays, and they went out for pizza and a movie, something Ashe's surveillance had probably noted.

"If she hasn't missed me yet, she will soon," Kori insisted. "She'll file a missing person's report."

"The cops don't pay any attention to missing adults for twenty-four hours."

"I'm not an adult," Kori whispered.

"*What*?" Promus's face was so close to Kori's she felt flecks of his spit on her cheek.

"I won't be eighteen until next month."

"Bitch! You lied to us!" His hand snaked out and slapped her face.

Kori pressed her tongue against the corner of her mouth and tasted blood. "I thought you knew! You seem to know everything else about me."

"This is a lucky break, Dad," said Scorch. "If it comes to prosecution, they'll go easy on a minor."

Promus turned his angry glare on Scorch. "No one's going to be prosecuted."

Kori got into bed fully clothed. She resolved to stay awake and when everyone else was asleep, she would creep down to the motel office and ask to use the phone. She lost that hope when Match and Scorch unrolled their sleeping bags, blocking the door.

The next morning, breakfast consisted of bananas, walnuts, and a gritty homemade granola.

Kori noticed she was the only one eating. "Isn't anyone else hungry?"

"We've got a breakfast meeting with some guys to go over the details of the mission," said Promus.

"I get to go!" Flicker said excitedly.

"And we need you to stay here to guard our stuff," Promus told Kori.

"What stuff? We can load it all in the car."

No one answered Kori. As Match, Scorch, and Flicker filed out of the room, Promus sat on his bed facing her.

"Why can't I go?" she asked.

"Trust in the Lord, my daughter. There are things about the mission it's better you don't know yet."

Flicker was the loud mouth, the fumbler. Why did she get to know stuff that Kori didn't? Probably the main reason she was allowed to go was to keep the two girls apart. Kori glared defiantly at Promus. "As soon as you drive off, I'm going right down to the office and call my mom."

"No, Kindle, you won't. I forbid you, and you must obey me. Don't leave the room. Speak to no one. And no TV."

"Why no TV?"

"You've got work to do." He dropped in her lap a thick, spiral-bound document entitled *The Armageddon Manifesto.* "Check the grammar in this. I forget some of the comma rules and shit, and you're still in school."

"Just tell me what the mission is so all this will make sense to me."

He shook his head slowly. "Trust in St. Michael. Trust in God. Let us pray, Kindle." He took both her hands and bowed his head. "Dear God, bless my daughter, Kindle, and give her the courage to be silent so that we may carry out your work." He droned on and on, and as he did so, he began to squeeze and relax his hands. With each pulse, he pressed tighter. Kori tried to pull her hands away, but she couldn't, not even when his grip was light. "Come, spirit of Michael," he chanted over and over, until eventually she joined in.

Kori's throat felt dry and scratchy, but her soul felt calm and faithful. As Promus left the room, he took the "Do Not Disturb" sign to hang on the outside door handle.

Kori took a pencil out of her backpack and opened *The Armageddon Manifesto.* Its title page stated, "By Michael the Archangel as dictated to Promus." It was mind-numbing, with lots of run-on sentences Kori had to fix. The style was uneven. Sometimes it read like a modern text and other parts were like the King James Bible with a bunch of "Yeas," "thees," and "thous." When Kori tried to read through the page-long paragraphs, her eyes glazed over, and she had to backtrack. After a few hours, she was only on page eleven of 645. She flipped through and made random corrections every few pages so it would look as if she had read more.

She ate more fruit and nuts for lunch. She paced the room. She made a few more corrections in *The Armageddon Manifesto*. She began to skip whole clumps of pages until she got to the last section entitled "The Battle of Armageddon." It stated that Armageddon would commence on the vernal equinox of this year. This caused her to sit up and pay attention. Promus believed the world was going to end *in March*? For real? She read on. The preemptive strike would erupt in the main residence at Promisedland.

Her finger trailed under the words, "Yea, and if thee emerge from the flames, thou shalt be smelted into a steel blade of a sword of Christ, and thou shalt pierce the hearts of Satan and his minions."

Kori stopped reading and stared across the room. She had often heard Promus claim in his sermons that he knew when the world would end, but he had never disclosed it. Then she realized that he hadn't intended her to read this far into the document.

From ancient to modern times, many people had predicted the end of the world. Kori remembered when some old guy Harold Camping had prophesied "the Rapture" to occur on May 21, 2011. All the saved people were supposed to fly up into heaven, and then the earth would burn for five months. After school on the Friday before that date, kids had hugged each other good-bye and some were crying. Camping was wrong, of course, and her gut told her that Promus was also wrong. Kori believed he was a holy man and maybe he did have visions of an angel, but she couldn't accept that the world was going to end in a couple of months, its destruction beginning a few miles from her house.

She scanned the text and erased any pencil markings she had made beyond page one hundred. Her stomach growled. She was sick of apples and craved a real dinner. It was nearly nine. Maybe the others were already on the mission, Promus having decided not to trust her with "the secret." Could the mission be so public that it would be on the local news? Was that the real reason Promus didn't want her to watch TV?

Kori hit the power button on the remote and flipped through the channels. She found news, all right. It was about a seventeen-year-old girl, who had been abducted from a rural town in California's San Joaquin

Valley. A man posing as her brother had lead her out of her high school on Friday, around noon. The teen appeared to go willingly, stated the newscaster, but the identity of her companion was unknown. A description of Kori's clothes followed. She looked down to see that she was still wearing them.

Headlights raced across the flimsy motel room curtains. Quickly she switched off the TV, propped the manifesto on her knees, and sank against the pillows.

The four Wheelers entered the room with Flicker riding piggyback on Promus.

"Is the mission over?" Kori asked matter-of-factly.

Everyone laughed. Promus dropped Flicker onto the bed, and she giggled like a little girl. He looked on Kori fondly, stroking her hair. "We wouldn't have left you out, Kindle, my daughter. It's all set up. We head out at eleven. I'll bet you're hungry. Let's eat."

Promus took them to a casino, where they rode a glass elevator up to a fancy restaurant overlooking the lake. Everything on the menu was outrageously expensive, but Promus ordered lots of food and drink. A Keno girl in a black leather miniskirt and rhinestone-studded halter top came around with Keno cards. Promus kept winning and tipping the girl. After they ate, Scorch and Match wandered off to play some nearby slot machines, and Promus was so busy flirting with the hot Keno girl that he didn't notice Kori slip away to the bathroom while Flicker was using it.

When she entered the women's room, she found Flicker standing before the hand dryer. Her eyes widened when she saw Kori. Glancing over at several women who were fixing their hair and makeup at the sinks, she whispered, "Don't ask me anything," her voice slightly slurred from the wine she wasn't used to.

"I didn't say anything," Kori said innocently.

Flicker smiled her cute smile, the corners of her mouth turning up. "See you back at our table."

"No! Wait for me!" Kori went into a stall for a quick pee. When she came out, the other women were gone. Washing her hands, Kori asked, "Are you excited about the mission?"

"Yeah. It's going to be awesome. I just wish I could shoot. Then I could be the fire starter."

"I'll teach you. Maybe by next Winter Solstice you'll be ready."

"I mean I want to start the fire on this mission."

Kori's nape prickled. "We're starting a fire? Where?"

Flicker clapped her palm over her mouth, her eyes darting fearfully.

"What's going on?" Kori's hand closed like a claw on her arm.

Flicker struggled against her. "Kindle, you're hurting me."

"Who was at the meeting?"

"Ow! Let go, and I'll tell you." Kori released her, and Flicker rubbed where her grip had left a pink ring on her forearm. "The developer who's building that hotel and casino place is destroying God's earth. We're gonna burn him out. Promus calls it Armageddon practice."

"It's called arson! I'm not doing it!"

"Oh, God, I've opened my big trap again. Promus warned me you might be weak in spirit."

"Promus is insane!"

Flicker gasped. "Kindle, how can you blaspheme? He's the general of God's own arm—"

"You can't see how wrong this is because you're in love with him!"

Flicker's countenance blushed magenta. "Of course I love Real Fath—"

"*In* love, Chelsea. You *want* him and not as a Holy Vessel. It makes you sick to think of yourself as just one of the girls. No, you want him all to yourself. You want to be Mrs. Vincent Dower."

Flicker glared at Kori. "What if I do? Do you think Flame is a good wife to him? She fucks Ashe! Things were going great between me and Promus before you came along!"

"You can have him! Go visit him in prison!"

Flicker yanked Kori's hair, twisting it around her fist. "I'm telling Promus you want to blow the whole mission!"

"Go ahead, Chelsea! You've betrayed your own parents. Why would you care what he does to me?"

She released Kori's hair, her arms falling limply to her side. "Wait, I won't tell if you don't tell I blabbed about the mission."

"Count me out!" Kori dashed for the door and slammed into Scorch, who had just entered the women's room. He grabbed her shoulders and steered her back to their table, while Flicker followed, her head hanging.

Scorch sat Kori down next to Promus, while Flicker slumped into another chair.

"I caught them talking together," Scorch reported.

Kori leaned into Promus and stated plainly, "I'm not committing arson."

"Shh! Keep it down!" He scowled at Flicker, speaking in a low, menacing tone. "I wanted to make this easy for all of us, but I guess some little bitch couldn't keep her mouth shut. If you don't start this fire, Kindle, there'll be a little fire set back at your house. Aren't your adulteress mother and her philandering lover boy asleep in her bed right now? Disobey me, Kindle, and there will be nothing left of them but their charred carcasses."

Kori steeled herself against his false threats. He hadn't killed anybody yet, not that she knew. "You'll never get to them in time."

"Why do you think I left Ashe behind?" He leered at Kori, his dark eyes wide and bulging.

The room began to spin. Kori weaved and groaned. "I'm going to throw up!" She gagged and held her mouth. She dashed toward the women's room and reached the toilet just in time. She turned, secured the latch on the stall, and vomited again.

"Kindle, are you okay?" Beneath the stall door Kori could see Flicker's pitiful feet, balanced on the heels of her ugly, scuffed boots. "Come on out. I promised we'd meet the guys downstairs at the front entrance."

Kori wasn't coming out. She was going to stay put in that bathroom stall. She'd be willing to stay for hours. Promus and the others would have to leave without her. Flicker crawled under the stall panel and unlatched the door. At the sink, she stood by Kori while she rinsed her mouth. Flicker linked her arm through Kori's and led her through the restaurant to the elevator. They got in it alone and descended toward the first floor. Kori reached out and pressed the number five on the control panel.

"Just let me go, Chelsea."

"I'm Flicker! My mission is to escort you to the door. Promus told me if I messed up one more time, he'd hand me over to Satan at the Armageddon!"

The elevator opened on the fifth floor. Kori struggled to escape, but Flicker was stronger than she thought. She crossed her forearm over Kori's throat in a chokehold until the elevator doors closed again. Flicker released her and began to chant, "Come, spirit of Michael," as Kori coughed and gasped for breath.

When the elevator opened on the ground floor, Flicker clutched Kori's hand and dragged her past the gamblers crowding around the card tables and slot machines. Up ahead, Promus and the others were waiting for them at the door leading to the street. They would shove her into the car and drive her to a bluff above the construction zone. Promus would help her aim the shotgun holding the Dragon's Breath, his body pressed against hers as he forced her to pull the trigger. Kori opened her mouth to scream, but no sound came out. An invisible hand squeezed her vocal cords.

She and Flciker reached the alcove where Lake Tahoe T-shirts were sold. Flicker walked on one side of the counter, and Kori walked on the other. Their hands knocked against the barrier and fell apart.

"Kindle, what are you doing?" Flicker called out to her. "We don't have time to shop."

A salesgirl was folding T-shirts and placing them in cubbyholes according to size and style. Kori pulled some of them out and threw them on the floor. She shook others open and draped them over her shoulders and head.

"Hey, cut it out," said the girl. "Are you crazy?"

"She's just a little drunk." Flicker approached Kori, her hand outstretched, her eyes pleading. "Kindle, come on!"

And then, because Kori wasn't hidden well enough, she dropped to the carpet and pulled a circular rack of T-shirts over the top of herself.

Chapter Nineteen

"I bet you get tired of hearing about it," Kori said wearily.

"No, no. You need to talk about it, girl, you talk," replied Officer Huerta.

Kori was out on a ride-along, Saturday night, the weekend after the Tahoe fiasco. "I feel like such an idiot!"

"You're our hero," said Huerta. "You stopped Dower from committing arson."

Kori liked it when Huerta used Promus's given name. It reduced him from a holy man to a low-life criminal. When the Tahoe police had rescued her in the T-shirt section of the casino, they notified the Goldhurst P.D. that she had been found. When she returned home, she told Huerta everything she knew about "the mission." Promus had aborted it, and when the police took him into custody, he claimed that he had never left Promisedland, and that Kori, Flicker, Scorch, and Match—aka Travis Collins and Joseph Mattingly—were merely proselytizing in the Tahoe area. At the time of his questioning, Flicker, Scorch, and Match were still on the road, so it was suspected that Promus hired a private plane home from the South Lake Tahoe airport to Meadows Field in Bakersfield. There was a record of such a flight, but the pilot claimed he had no passengers, just cargo.

"No conviction, though," Kori said dejectedly.

"True, but we know for sure something we've always suspected: Dower is an arsonist."

"His word against mine," said Kori. The district attorney had no evidence to prosecute, so Promus had been released after questioning.

"Yeah, right. Religious persecution," Huerta retorted sarcastically. That was what Promus had claimed to the media. "How's your mom doing?"

"Oh, she's so happy I quit the Wheel she's forgiven me for everything. She doesn't like to be lied about, though." Travis Collins had claimed Cindy Lawton had given him permission to take Kori out of school.

"And you?"

Kori sighed. Her week back at school had been rough. Kids stared at her a lot and pointed fingers. Bitsy and her group had asked her a lot of embarrassing questions, not because they cared about her, she felt, but so they could talk smack about her behind her back. She and Luke had texted back and forth, but she hadn't yet had the courage to meet him face-to-face. She yearned to return to the relationship they'd had before she joined the Wheel, but she was afraid Luke was too hurt to give her a second chance.

Kori sighed heavily. "I just want my old life back." They passed China-To-Go, reminding her of her first meeting with Flicker. Everyone she loved had warned her against getting involved with a Wheel member, but she had charged ahead heedlessly. "I was determined to get Flicker and Mrs. Jamison out of the Wheel, but instead, I got sucked in!"

"You're out now. That's the important thing. Think of it as a learning experience."

"Yes, ma'am. I learned I'm a weak, gullible fool."

"Now, now. You learned there's such a thing as mind control, and it's a powerful force. You know about that Elizabeth Smart, right? When a detective walked right up to her in a public library and asked her who she was, she used the name her abductor had given her. In a matter of weeks he had convinced her she was a completely different person."

Kori thought about the girl on Winter Solstice who had fired a shotgun without even knowing its ammunition, the same girl who had walked on live coals. That girl wasn't her, Kori Lawton, but another girl, Kindle—no one now, but an embarrassing, painful memory.

Officer Huerta nudged her with an elbow. "Hey, did you hear they're thinking of changing the name of the AMBER Alert to the Kori Alert?"

"Very funny." Kori was forced to smile, which made her feel a little better.

The traffic light in front of the hospital changed to yellow, and Huerta pumped the brake. In the rearview mirror, Kori saw that the female driver of the car behind them didn't intend to stop. Her male passenger crossed his forearms over his face anticipating the impact, but in the nick of time the driver swerved around the cruiser and streaked into the intersection as cross traffic entered it. Brakes screeched and horns blared, as the speeding vehicle, a gray compact, turned left into the hospital parking lot.

"Plate number!" Huerta ordered as she hit her lights and siren.

Reaching for her bag, Kori exclaimed, "It must be an emergency!"

"That's no excuse to kill a bunch of other people on the way! Did you get the license?"

Kori mouthed the letters and numbers as she got out her pen and notepad to write them down. Huerta wove through the cars stalled in the intersection and turned into the hospital. The gray car was up ahead, parked at the emergency room entrance. A man whose face was concealed in an oversized hoodie was out of the car, pulling a bundle out of the backseat, the size and shape of a human being. He deposited his load on the pavement, rolled it to the curb, and then leaped into the backseat as the driver sped off.

"Did you get a good look at them?" Huerta asked.

"Yes, ma'am. I know them. They're Wheelers." Kori didn't recognize the gray car, but she could swear the driver was Flame and the man was probably Ashe.

Huerta and Kori leaped out of the cruiser to inspect the person they had dumped. Matted, gray-streaked, black hair tumbled out of the top of a sleeping bag. Huerta pushed the fabric down to reveal the strained face of a middle-aged female. She pressed her fingers to the woman's throat, searching for a pulse.

"It's Luke's mom! Is she alive?" Kori asked.

"Barely."

Two orderlies dashed out of the door with a gurney.

"You say the suspects are Wheelers?" Huerta asked. "Let's go."

"Can I identify them later? I want to stay with Mrs. Jamison."

Huerta looked into Kori's pleading eyes. "All right."

As Officer Huerta drove off, Kori texted Luke that his mom had been dropped off at the emergency room. When the orderlies lifted Mrs.

Jamison onto the gurney, she moaned faintly, seeming to drift in and out of consciousness. As Kori walked alongside the gurney, she noticed her opening and closing her fingers. Kori slipped her hand into hers, and Mrs. Jamison continued the motion, sending weak pulses as she squeezed back. Kori hoped it wasn't too late for their prayers.

As an ER doctor walked toward them, one of the orderlies said, "Abandoned patient."

The doctor slowed.

"I know her!" Kori said. "Her family can pay."

"Then why'd they dump her?"

"They didn't. She's been…away."

"Alcoholic? Junkie?" asked the doctor.

Kori shook her head. "She's a Wheel member, Maureen Jamison. Her husband will be here soon."

"There's the waiting room," said one of the orderlies, pointing to the right.

"Can't I stay with her?" Kori asked.

"We'll notify you when she's able to see visitors," said the doctor.

Kori's fingers slipped from Mrs. Jamison's as they wheeled her away. A few feet down the hall, a piece of debris fluttered from her sleeping bag. Kori loped up to retrieve it. She settled in the waiting room. In about twenty minutes, Luke showed up. She ran to him and fell into his outstretched arms.

"How is she?" he murmured against her hair.

"Alive!" She shuddered and clung to him, melting into his warm embrace. "Getting the care she needs. That bastard Vincent Dower should be charged with medical neglect!"

"Not Promus?"

She held his face in her hands, peering into the deep pools of his eyes, made bluer by the black of his rippling hair. "Oh, Luke! I've been such a dumb ass! Can you forgive me?"

"Missed you, babe. Missed you a lot!"

"I'm back, Luke. Me—the real Kori. I'm yours if you'll have me."

He smiled ruefully and kissed her parted lips.

"Where's your dad?" she asked.

"Looking for someone to stay with the kids."

"You should have done that. He should be here."

His mouth tightened. "I tried to tell him that. But anything that has to do with my mom is hard for him. How'd she get here?"

Kori explained how she and Officer Huerta had been cruising by the hospital when they saw Flame and Ashe dump his mom at the emergency entrance.

"They couldn't even be bothered admitting her," Luke said bitterly.

He went to the admittance window and returned with a stack of forms on a clipboard. He began to write in the information he knew and left blank what his dad would have to enter later. As he bent over his work, Kori gazed down the hall where they had wheeled away his mom.

"What's that?" Luke was staring at her hand.

"Oh, it's you. The photo I gave your mom when I first met her in Promisedland. It looks like she wore it out holding on to it."

He leaned into her, his cheek moist with tears. "You did it, babe. You got my mom back. You said you were going to, and you did, even after I gave up."

"It wasn't my doing."

"Yes, it was," he insisted and kissed her brow. "My brave girl, who never gives up on what's right."

Mr. Jamison arrived, his weathered face creased with concern. He thanked Kori for notifying Luke, but didn't have much else to say. About an hour later, the doctor appeared to deliver his diagnosis: double pneumonia, malnutrition, and dehydration.

"Is she going to pull through?" Mr. Jamison asked bluntly.

"We can hope," the doctor answered tersely. "We're admitting her to ICU."

"Can we see her?" asked Luke.

"For a short visit," said the doctor.

"You two go on," said Mr. Jamison. "I've got to get back to the kids."

Kori and Luke said their good-byes and watched him walk away. "Do you think that's weird?" she asked.

Luke raised his eyebrows. "Doesn't surprise me. It's just the way he feels about my mom right now."

Maureen Jamison spent nearly a week in the hospital before she was released to go home, still weak and underweight, but recovering. She moved into Grace and Terry's bedroom, which hadn't been used since the sisters had gone to live with Maureen's sister, Mary. Billy and Lizzie had no recollection of their mother and referred to her as "that sick lady." Mr. Jamison and Luke did what they could to make her comfortable, but it was Connor who was in his mother's room nearly every moment he was home, reading to her, playing endless games of Crazy Eights, but mainly just *being* with the mother he had missed so much. Kori visited her nearly every day. Mrs. Jamison insisted that she call her "Maureen" while Kori still called her husband "Mr. Jamison," which felt kind of awkward.

The same week that the daffodils sprouted in buttery patches all over the Jamisons's backyard, Maureen got out of bed and assumed the role of the mother of a large household. The kids got used to her presence, and within a couple of weeks Billy and Lizzie were calling her Mommy. On one of her trips into town, she had her hair dyed black and cropped so that it curled over her shoulders. She replaced her long skirts for jeans and looked years younger.

One Sunday morning, Maureen dressed the little kids and fixed their hair, and the Jamison family attended Valley Community Church. Kori accompanied them, and while it wasn't anything like the wildly ecstatic Wheel rituals, she liked the congregational singing and the relaxed manner of Pastor Schuller, who kept his sermon brief and free of hellfire.

After the service, they spoke to Mary and her family, the Bentleys, outside the church. Besides taking care of Gracie and Terry, they had two little boys of their own. Terry, who was twelve, had auburn hair and freckles and looked like her dad. Gracie, a year older, was the beauty. She took after Maureen, except that her wide eyes were hazel, nearly green. Terry ran up to her mom and hugged her. Her dad scooped her up in his arms like she was a much younger child. Gracie, meanwhile, hung back, leaning against her Aunt Mary and staring warily at her parents.

"We'll be making arrangements to move the girls home as soon as possible," said Maureen.

"Oh, there's no rush," said Mary, who wore high spiky heels and complicated big hair. "You'll want to get stronger before taking on another two kids."

"I'm strong enough now," Maureen said in a firm, even voice.

A sneer settled into the corners of Mary's small, pert mouth. "We'll see about that. You haven't been all that strong in the past."

Maureen met her sister's eyes. "The past is over."

That week Terry returned home to her old bedroom, while Gracie begged to remain with her aunt. Maureen moved into the master bedroom, and Mr. Jamison took the den.

Before Kori and their children, Andy and Maureen Jamison were overly polite like people who didn't know each other very well. Luke confided to Kori that he often heard them arguing in hushed voices at night behind the closed door of the master bedroom. Mr. Jamison wanted a separation, although neither he nor Maureen was willing to move out. "I would never desert my children," he argued bitterly.

As for Flame and Ashe being prosecuted for dumping Maureen at the emergency room, both of them had alibis, seen by over a hundred Wheelers at a service at the time of the drop-off. The license plate number of the car was traced to a Wheel member, Ralph Bannister. He and his wife Trudie had attended the service that evening, but both of them swore that they had not left Promisedland until an hour after the time of the incident. Without any hard evidence, charges against Flame and Ashe were dropped. The good thing was that Maureen Jamison lived.

Chapter Twenty

The next Sunday morning, Kori attended church with the Jamisons again. Annie was thrilled to have her big sister, Terry, living at home and insisted on braiding her hair. The braids turned out lopsided, with loose strands of hair sticking out, but Terry claimed Annie had done a great job. After the service, Mr. Jamison made a huge breakfast of bacon, eggs, and pancakes. The kids ate quickly and left the table, but Kori, Luke, and his parents lingered over their coffee.

"I about died laughing at the look on Mary's face when she saw Terry's hair," said Maureen. "I bet she thought I had braided it."

"I'd like to know when Grace is coming home," Mr. Jamison said gruffly.

"Give her some time, Andy," Maureen said. "She'll come around."

An orange Wheel of Fire van pulled into the Jamisons's driveway, Ashe in the driver's seat, Flame next to him, and some other members seated in back.

"Pack your bags, Maureen," Mr. Jamison said coldly. "Your family is here to claim you."

Luke jumped to his feet to peer out the kitchen window. "Hell, I'll get my rifle!"

Mr. Jamison caught his arm. "Calm down, son. You'll do no such thing."

Maureen said nothing, but when she raised her mug to her lips, her hand trembled.

The front doorbell sounded, and Connor dashed into the living room to answer it.

"Don't open the door," Luke exclaimed. "It's bad people who want to steal Mom away."

Connor leaped from the door, his mouth gaping.

"Let's invite our *guests* in," Mr. Jamison said in a steely voice, his narrowed eyes challenging Maureen. He opened the door. "Well, well, what a surprise!" he said sarcastically. "Come in! Come in!"

Flame's appearance had transformed since Kori had seen her last. Her face seemed bigger and brighter, and she wasn't as thin.

Ashe, Roberta, Rayann, and Flicker followed her into the house. Mr. Jamison shut the door behind them, and they all stood in an awkward cluster in the entrance hall.

Rayann, with the burden of her dowager's hump, stooped forward as she shuffled toward Maureen. "We've been so worried about you, Ember. How are you feeling?"

"Much better, thank you."

"We've come to take you home, dear," said Roberta.

Maureen raised her chin. "I am home."

"Your real home," said Flicker, offering her a light, quick embrace, "with your Real Father!"

Luke shoved his palm against Ashe's shoulder. "You're not welcomed in this house! You ditched my mom in the gutter to die."

"Son!" Maureen said gently. "Flame and Ashe saved my life. It was Promus who left me to die in a dark, unheated room."

Flame blushed a glowing fuchsia. "That isn't true, Ember. If you had died it would have been God's will, and obviously it wasn't. God has brought you back from death's door to test your faith. You'll be whole again when you return to your real family."

"Praise God!" shouted Flicker, leaping gingerly on the balls of her injured feet. "Praise Michael the Archangel!"

"I left my children once. I'll never do it again," said Maureen.

"Witness this man," said Flame, pointing to Mr. Jamison. "It's plain he doesn't want you here. There's no home for you, except with your real family, Wheel of Fire in Promisedland."

"Get the hell out!" yelled Luke, flinging open the door.

"We need to hear that from Ember," Ashe challenged him.

"You heard my son," Maureen said serenely.

Flame lunged forward, grasped both of Maureen's hands and began to squeeze rhythmically, searching her eyes.

Maureen met her gaze. "I see that congratulations are in order, Sharon." Flame's hands stopped moving; her lips parted. Maureen smiled at her sweetly, her lashes fluttering. "Well, you are expecting, aren't you? Don't let Vince talk you out of this one." Maureen held her palm flat against Flame's abdomen. "Fight for you child."

Flame backed away and scurried out the door, her head bowed. The other Wheel members filed after her, Flicker last in line. She paused before Kori, her eyes crinkling at the corners. "Real Father has forgiven you, Kindle! He understands you were weak in spirit. You must return to us!"

How could Promus possibly forgive her for the trouble she had caused him in Tahoe? It was obviously a trap. Kori looked fondly upon the sweet, lost girl she would never be able to save. "I'm done."

"But I'm so lonely without you. I've got loads to tell you!" Flicker caught her hand and squeezed it. When she let go, Kori held an orange sticky note in her palm. As Luke slammed the front door behind the departing Wheelers, Kori glanced down to read, "Meet me at China-To-Go, Wed at 4."

"What's that?" asked Luke.

"Garbage." Kori wadded the note up and threw it in the trash under the kitchen sink. When she returned to the living room, everyone was tense and silent.

"Took you long enough to choose between us and Promus, your prophet," Mr. Jamison accused Maureen.

"I never believed in Promus!"

"Like hell!" said Mr. Jamison.

"I better go," Kori murmured.

"No, stay," said Maureen. "I want you to hear this."

"Who's Promus?" asked Connor.

"I'll tell you later, sweetie," said Maureen, steering the boy by the shoulders out of the room. "You go watch TV with the other kids." She returned to sit with Mr. Jamison, Luke, and Kori. "You know, Andy, I've suffered from depression."

He nodded. "I do."

"You know, after each baby was born, my mind would grow blacker and blacker. Lizzie was the worst."

"You had your medication."

She shrugged. "It didn't really help. I tried to explain it to you. The afternoon I left, Lizzie wouldn't stop crying. I rocked her, I walked her, I fed her, I burped her. Nothing worked. Finally I set her down in her crib. She cried even harder. I screamed at her to shut up. I grabbed a pillow... and..." Her voice broke into a hoarse whisper. "I took the pillow and pushed it over her face."

Mr. Jamison gasped. Maureen dropped her head into her hands, her shoulders trembling. A long moment passed before she looked up. "I never intended to hurt her, but my actions shocked and frightened me. I lifted the pillow and ran out the door. Lizzie was safe in her crib, Billy and Annie were okay in the backyard, and soon Connor and Luke would be home from school."

"I never realized you were having so much trouble," said Mr. Jamison.

"Oh, Andy, I tried to tell you! Many times. You said my 'moods' would pass. I wasn't suicidal, and yet I feared our children weren't safe around me. I got in the car and drove, not knowing where I was going. When I reached Promisedland, I turned in. I thought it was a place where I could stay and rest, just for a few days. Of course Promus interrogated me. He made me confess what I had done, and then he convinced me that I had indeed tried to murder my own child. Lizzie's life was never in danger, I'm sure of that now, but Promus convinced me it was. He said if I ever tried to return home, you would have me arrested and put in jail. He forced me to believe I could never leave Promisedland."

"And now?" asked Mr. Jamison.

"I'm not depressed anymore. I'm well, and I'm hoping it's not too late for us all to be a family again. For God's sake, Andy, give me a chance to make it up to you and the kids."

Mr. Jamison walked over to his wife and placed his hand on her cheek. "I can try, Maureen," he said at last.

She covered his hand with hers. "That's all I'm asking."

Mr. Jamison looked into her face a moment longer, then walked into the back porch to put on his work clothes.

Luke hugged his mom. "I...didn't know."

"How could you, dear? Thank you for caring for your sisters and brothers while I was gone. I'm back now, son."

Luke grinned and kissed her cheek. "Dad wants me to help him clear that brush this morning."

"Go on. I want to talk to Kori."

When Luke left, Kori said, "I have so many questions,"

"I'll answer any of them I can. Let's go for a walk." As they strolled down the dirt path leading to the walnut orchards, Maureen linked her arm with Kori's.

"You never believed in Promus?" Kori asked.

She shook her head, smiling faintly. "No."

"I did. I feel ridiculous! I'm so ashamed for begging money for him. And yet, something amazing happened to me the night of Winter Solstice. I'll never forget it. What did happen to me?"

"What do you think?"

"I thought–I was told–that I was engulfed by a holy spirit. It was the greatest feeling I've ever had in my whole life!"

"Then hold on to that feeling."

"It's gone, but I do have faith in God. A calm, peaceful faith. Everything in the Wheel was so intense. I don't think I ever got a flame over my head, though."

Maureen laughed. "That's because you weren't inside where the lights are rigged."

"Oh!" Kori sighed. "Then everything about the Wheel is fake?"

"Not everything. The power of prayer is real. So is God."

"Faith is so confusing!"

"Of course! Why do you think there are so many religions in the world? Why do you think that there are maniacs who behead people in the name of God?"

"Now that I'm out of the Wheel, I just can't imagine how anyone could believe in Promus. All that stuff about fighting in fire at Armageddon—it terrified me."

"Promus controls people through fear. Basically he's harmless, like a little boy who plays with matches."

"Oh, no. After being on that so-called mission, I know he can be dangerous."

Maureen coughed and clutched her chest.

"Are you okay?" Kori asked.

"Oh, yes, better every day."

"I'm sorry you got so sick."

"I'm not! That's how I found my way back to my family. You see, Kori? The Lord does provide, even in sickness!" She stopped on the path and her neck arched so that she peered straight to the sky. "Ah, it's a wonderful world! It feels great to be home!" She hugged Kori. "Thank you for this."

"I didn't do anything!"

"You did. You handed me Luke's picture. You got me thinking that returning to my family was a possibility. Without you, dear girl, I probably would've died of despair."

Chapter Twenty-One

Done! Done! Done! No way was Kori ever going to communicate with a Wheel member again, not even Flicker. And yet here she was, four o'clock, Wednesday, at China-To-Go, at the meeting Flicker had requested on the orange sticky note she had slipped her. Kori had arrived early to order Flicker's favorite, sweet and sour pork. There it was waiting for her, hot and tempting on an outside table, when Flicker walked up, smiling brightly, her eyes crinkled, her mouth turned up at the corners. She had the same oversized clothes, chapped lips, and straw hair, and yet she looked different—happy, almost glowing. "Hey," she said almost shyly, swinging her leg over the bench to sit across from Kori.

"Hey." Kori pushed the food toward her.

"Oh, no thanks. I'm sticking to my raw food diet."

"Oh, well." Kori looked over her shoulder warily. She had an uneasy feeling she was being set up. "Where's the other three horsemen?"

"I'm alone."

"That's allowed?"

"Yeah. Real Father asked me to talk to you. We all feel terrible that you completely misunderstood the mission."

"I can tell you it had nothing to do with saving God's green earth. Vincent Dower was hired—"

"Who?" Flicker squinted and cocked her head.

"Have it your way. Promus was hired to burn out the construction site for a cut of the insurance, probably worth millions."

Flicker nodded. For an instant, Kori thought she was agreeing with her. "That's just what Real Father told me you'd say."

"Because I'm right, and he knows it."

"There's lies about Real Father swarming all around us. He was only—"

"Let's agree to disagree," Kori interrupted good-naturedly. From her backpack she removed a leftover piece of birthday cake. "Will you be able to resist this?"

"Oh! Happy Birthday! You're legal now."

"Yup! I got my CCW in the mail today. I've been wanting to go to the shooting range with my handgun, and now I can. Here, try a bite. It's chocolate with raspberry filling."

Flicker eyed the cake longingly. "No thanks! I'm trying to be pure."

"Since when?"

"Since Real Father awarded me with a special title!"

"Congratulations! What is it?"

"I can't tell, but he's being so sweet to me. He dropped all kidnapping charges against my parents. You know how lawsuits drag on. We're already in End Time. And I got permission to go home to meet my new baby niece, Chelsea."

"She's already born! When?"

"March seventeenth."

"That's *my* birthday!"

"I know! Too bad she won't even live a year. Real Father is planning the Armageddon for summer solstice."

"No one can *plan* the Armageddon. No one but God."

Flicker's brow creased. "That's what I thought he said. Maybe he meant plan *for* it. The angel told him the date long ago, and he revealed it to all of us Wheelers just this week." She slapped her hand over he mouth. "I probably shouldn't have told you."

"I already read about it. Remember? Promus had me proofread *The Armageddon Manifesto.*" What Kori had read, however, did not agree with what Flicker was telling her. In his document, Promus had predicted Armageddon to fall on the vernal equinox, not the summer solstice. He was the one making up the rules; he could change them if he wanted. "Just because Promus says the Armageddon is going to happen at a certain time doesn't make it true. I bet little Chelsea will live to be an old woman."

Flicker's countenance turned impassive. "I should go."

"Hey, chill. We're just talking here. Tell me about your special title."

"I'm sworn to secrecy!" She dragged a finger across the cake icing and popped it into her mouth. "Not even the other Wheelers can know about it, not even Ashe and Flame!"

An alarm was sounding in Kori's head. It must be something they wouldn't approve of, like "the mission." "You can tell me," she coaxed. "I won't tell anybody."

Grinning, Flicker blurted, "I'm the Messenger Angel!"

Kori leaned into her. "Humans can turn into angels?"

"Not a real angel. It's just my title. After Armageddon is over, I get to proclaim Promus as General of the Christian army."

"Oh. Great." Kori didn't want to squash Flicker's happiness, but at the same time she wanted to give her something to think about. "I don't get it. Who are you going to proclaim it to? Like, won't the world be gone? Won't everybody be dead?"

Flicker shoveled a big bite of cake into her mouth and chewed thoughtfully. "To tell you the truth, I'm not sure how it will work. Maybe I'll go around heaven proclaiming it to the faithful."

"Won't they already know?" Kori suppressed a laugh, which erupted like a snort. "Maybe you'll be sent to hell to tell everybody down there."

Flicker turned to leave, but Kori grabbed her wrist. It wasn't funny, not a bit of it, but Kori was trying so hard not to laugh that tears were spurting from her eyes. Promus's bullshit sounded so ridiculous now that she no longer believed it. "Let's talk about something else. What else is new at Promisedland?"

"What goes on in Promisedland, stays in Promisedland."

"I don't mean to pry." Kori slid the cake closer to her and handed her a plastic fork. "'I'm just wondering how everyone is doing—Roberta and Rayann and Stix and—"

"Promus kicked Stix out!"

"Whoa! How come?"

Flicker peered around to be certain she wouldn't be overheard and lowered her voice. "You were there the day Stix first saw Michael the Archangel, right? Well, he's seen him more times. The angel told Stix different stuff than what he told Promus, and that really pissed him off."

"I get it. No room at the top for a second leader. Where's Stix now?"

"Not sure. He hiked out of Promisedland with a few provisions last week, and hasn't been heard from since."

"That's a story! Do you think he's okay?"

"There's rumors that he might start his own branch of the Wheel." Flicker rolled her eyes. "There's not much time for that."

"When are you going to L.A. to see baby Chelsea?"

"Next week. I'm trying to line up public transportation, but it's really complicated from Goldhurst: bus, train, bus, another train."

"Hey, next week is spring break. Do you think Promus would let me drive you? I'd like to meet baby Chelsea, too."

"Hmm…I'll ask." Flicker speared another morsel of cake and popped it in her mouth, a dab of icing dotting her upper lip.

Within the hour, Flicker texted Kori, "It's OK. Promus says I can go with you."

At the dinner table that evening, Kori waited until Vaughn made his usual trip to the bathroom, before she explained the situation to her mom. "Can I take Flicker to see her niece?"

"If you are really driving her to her parents house in Marina Del Rey—yes. If any other Wheeler shows up and tries to talk you into doing something else, you come straight home!"

Kori nodded. "Agreed. I think it will be okay, Mom."

"I hope so."

"Hope what?" asked Vaughn returning to the kitchen.

Cindy grinned at him. "None of your bee's wax."

Kori was looking forward to the road trip with Flicker, but as the day grew closer she found herself more and more uneasy. She had caused Promus a lot of trouble, even got him arrested. And wasn't he the least bit afraid Flicker would decide to stay with her parents and never return to him? Was it possible that he was scheming some weird shit mission that he was going to spring on them the last minute? The whole setup felt wrong.

The morning of the trip, after Kori packed, said good-bye to her mom, and threw her overnight bag in the bed of her truck, she returned to the house.

Cindy looked up from her computer in the kitchen alcove. "Forget something?"

"I think." Kori stood in the middle of her bedroom for several minutes before she took out her Glock, loaded it, and stowed it in the pouch of her hoodie. "Bye again," she called to her mom as she dashed out the back door, jumped in her truck, and placed the gun in the glove box.

Having refused to pick up Flicker at Promisedland, she drove into town to their meeting spot at China-To-Go. Flicker tossed her duffle in the back and got into the cab. Kori steered her truck onto Highway 99, and away they went.

"Hey, Promus let me take one of the Wheel's cell phones! I've never been trusted with a phone all to myself." Flicker took it out of her pocket and began fiddling with it. "How do you get Internet on this thing?"

"Let me see." Kori checked it out quickly. "You don't have Internet."

"What about games?"

"I'll see. Nope. No apps at all. I've never seen a phone this stripped down." Kori handed it back to her. "You might as well have a walkie-talkie."

"Oh, pooh!" Flicker continued to play with the phone.

Kori's text message signal chimed. "That must be Luke." She glanced at the message. It said, "Hi."

Flicker howled with delight as if she had pulled a clever prank.

"Messing with a cell phone while driving causes accidents," Kori lectured.

"Sorry. Just practicing."

When they drove a little farther, Flicker asked, "Can we stop at a burger place for lunch?"

"I thought you were eating pure."

"I am." Flicker grinned sheepishly. "When I get back to Promisedland."

"Cool. Let's live it up on this trip."

After feasting on a hamburger, fries, and shake, Flicker patted her concave abdomen. "If I ate like this all the time, I'd be fat."

"Which reminds me, when you guys came over Luke's house, I happened to notice Flame has quite the tummy on her. She looks—"

"Right. Preggers."

"Is Promus going to force her to terminate?"

Flicker shook her head. "There's no time for the baby to be born."

Kori was silent a moment before deciding to take the risk of pissing Flicker off. "Do you think it bothers Promus that his wife is carrying another man's baby?"

Flicker shrugged. "He and Flame are pretty much just business partners. They sure have been arguing a lot lately."

"About the baby?"

"I don't know, but with them fighting and Stix getting kicked out, and Armageddon coming up, things are pretty tense around Promisedland. I'm glad to get away for a few days."

Kori got back on the freeway. Several minutes passed before she got another text. It read, "Hi."

"Cut it out!" she said, but she laughed along with Flicker.

Kori and Flicker enjoyed three fun days in Marina del Rey. Flicker's parents had promised not to pressure her about getting out of the Wheel, and they kept their word. Flicker spent a lot of time holding her baby niece Chelsea and singing at the piano with Melanie. When anyone addressed Flicker as Chelsea, she didn't seem to mind. Mrs. Cunningham made her favorite dishes, and at each meal she ate until she groaned.

On the last day of their visit, they were scheduled to leave in the afternoon. At breakfast, Flicker began to cry. She wiped her tears with a napkin and blew her nose.

"Honey, what's the matter?" asked Mrs. Cunningham. "You don't have to leave, you know."

Flicker shook her head. "This is probably the last time I'll ever see you."

"Why?" asked Mrs. Cunningham. "Are you being forced to take a Shunning Vow again?"

"The world is going to end and soon! Please, Mom and Dad, join the Wheel so we can rise up to heaven together after Armageddon."

"We'll be saved," Mrs. Cunningham said calmly. "We're Christians."

"That's not enough," argued Flicker. "You have to believe that Promus is General of God's army. You have to become a soldier of Christ and fight in the Armageddon."

Mr. Cunningham stirred his coffee so vigorously it lapped over the edge of his cup. "I doubt if Judgment Day will come during our lifetime."

"Oh, but it will!" said Flicker. "It's coming on summer solstice! The prophet Promus has decreed it!"

Mr. Cunningham threw down his spoon with a clatter. "Promus is a charlatan! He's stolen your life, Chelsea. We've tried to make you see that."

"You'll come with me, won't you, Mom? Please!" Flicker gripped her mother's upper arms and shook her.

"Let go, Chelsea! You're hurting me!"

"Stop!" Mr. Cunningham lunged across the table to pry Flicker's hands away. In the struggle, the coffee pot tipped over, the hot liquid scalding Mrs. Cunningham's lap. She leaped up, screaming in pain, trying to hold the steaming cloth of her slacks away from her body.

"Now look what you've done!" Mr. Cunningham yelled at Flicker. "Haven't you made your mother and I suffer enough?"

"Oh, Mom, I'm sorry!" Flicker dashed to the refrigerator, but Mr. Cunningham shoved her aside. He opened the freezer and dumped ice cubes into a plastic bag as Mrs. Cunningham whimpered.

"I'll call 911," said Flicker.

"Never mind," shouted Mr. Cunningham. "Driving to the ER is quicker." He held the plastic bag to his wife thighs and led her toward the garage.

Flicker opened the car door for her. "We'll come, too,"

"No, you won't!" Mr. Cunningham retorted bitterly. "I want you cleared out of here by the time we get back. Go on, run back to your cult! I'm sick of looking at you, *Flicker.* Our daughter is dead to us."

"Oh, Ted, don't tell her that!" Mrs. Cunningham exclaimed, sobbing and looking longingly at Flicker.

Mr. Cunningham climbed into the car and backed out of the garage.

Flicker slumped against Kori, crying. "Do you think my mom will be okay?"

"I hope so."

"What can I do for her?"

"Your dad's pretty mad. We better leave."

Kori and Flicker packed their things and loaded the truck. On the drive home, Flicker called and texted her dad's phone several times, but he wouldn't answer. "I was only trying to save them!"

"I know, I know." Kori patted her shoulder.

They were on the road about two hours when Kori got a text. She pulled her phone out of her bag and handed it to Flicker. "What's it say?"

"It's from Luke. He says, 'Happy Spring.'"

"Oh, that's right. Today's the first day of spring. Write back, 'You too, babe. See you soon.'"

Flicker sent the text and dropped Kori's phone back in her bag.

They were about fifteen miles south of Goldhurst when Flicker got a text message on her phone. "It's from Promus," she said. "Oh my God, listen to this!" She read, "'Leave now. Return home, Messenger Angel, to chronicle our holy battle. Armageddon has begun!'" Flicker pressed her hand to her forehead. "This can't be happening! It's too soon!"

"The vernal equinox!" Kori exclaimed. "In his manifesto, Promus wrote that Armageddon would begin *today*!"

"That's wrong! Over and over, he preached to the Wheel that *summer solstice* is the starting day! That's all he's talked about for the last two weeks."

"Maybe he didn't want to alarm anyone." Kori looked in the rearview mirror, and when it was safe, she pulled off the freeway and took out her phone.

"Who are you calling?" asked Flicker.

"Officer Huerta."

"You think the cops can stop Armageddon?"

"They can try." Kori told Huerta about Promus's message.

"We've got a big meth bust going on in town," she said. "I'll drive out to Promisedland when I can get away."

"Hurry!" Kori told her. "I think something terrible is about to happen."

Chapter Twenty-Two

Smoke darkened the sky; flames leaped above the treetops.

"It's started," shouted Flicker, bouncing in the passenger seat of Kori's truck. "The Armageddon has started! Quick! Whose side will you take, Kindle? God or Satan's?"

Kori concentrated on careering down Blue Ridge Road as fast as possible without missing a curve. Behind her, sirens blared, forcing her to brake and pull onto the shoulder. In her rearview mirror, she looked for an opening. An ambulance, a sheriff, and two fire trucks roared by. Just as she rolled back onto the pavement, an oncoming black Mercedes swung wide, nearly plowing into her truck. The driver braked, fought for control of the skidding vehicle, and then accelerated out of sight around the next bend.

"Wow, that was close!" Kori tightly gripped the wheel. "Was that Promus?"

"Looked like his car, but no way would he be fleeing the Armageddon. Did you see who was driving?"

"Nope! I was concentrating on not getting hit."

The emergency vehicles sped past the entrance to Promisedland, heading another quarter mile up the road to the abandoned packinghouse, which was engulfed in flames.

"Whoa, if Armageddon was supposed to start at Promisedland, it kinda missed," Kori said.

"This is no time for joking!" Flicker snapped.

The gate to Promisedland was open. Kori steered up the private road and skidded to a halt in front of the ranch house. The property looked deserted, except for Promus, who was pouring liquid from a large gasoline can on hay, which had been strewn around the perimeter of the big house. His head jerked up from his task, and he did not look happy to see them. Flicker leaped out of the truck.

"No, Flicker, wait!" Kori called after her, but she was already bounding toward Promus like a puppy dog delighted to see its master.

"How the hell did you get here so fast?" he yelled at her.

"We were already on our way home."

Kori reached into her glove box, removed her Glock, and placed it in the small of her back under her sweatshirt before getting out of the truck.

"Where is everyone?" asked Flicker.

"Inside. The Armageddon is about to commence." Promus withdrew a long-barreled lighter from his back pocket, flicked it on, and touched it to the gasoline-soaked hay. A wheel of fire traversed around the large structure.

Kori drew her gun and dashed toward the house to shoot off the lock on the wrought iron grill baring the front door. His wild eyes rolling in their sockets, Promus stepped into her path, kicked the gun out her hand, and wrenched her arms behind her back.

"Flicker, pick up the gun," he ordered.

She obeyed without hesitation.

"Now shoot her! Walk up to her and placed the barrel against her heart. That way, you won't miss and fuck things up like you usually do."

"Shoot Kori?" Flicker looked from the gun to her friend.

Frantically, Kori shook her head, pleading with her eyes.

"Do as I say!" ordered Promus. "She's trying to stop the Armageddon! She's picked a side, and it's Satan's!"

"No, Flicker!" Kori yelled, struggling to squirm out of Promus's grip. "He's insane! He wants to murder everyone you love!"

Promus twisted Kori's arms forcefully so that she screamed in pain. She could smell his sour sweat and feel his body heaving against her back.

"Don't listen to this she-devil bitch, Flicker. Shoot her! Now!"

Flicker raised her arm and pointed the gun at Kori.

"That's right, Messenger Angel. You are the one who's going to tell the whole world what happened here under my glorious command. Now, shoot!"

With adrenaline coursing through her body, Kori stomped on Promus's foot with all her might. His hold on her slipped, and she whirled around and kicked him in the crotch. With a groan, he crumpled to the ground in a fetal position. Kori ran for her life, zigzagging as she went. Since Flicker had never fired a gun, there was a good chance she would miss her.

Kori heard the blast, but no bullet whizzed by her. Promus released an agonizing scream. She looked back. Flicker held the gun limply at her side, staring down at Promus writhing in the dirt, blood pulsing from the gaping wound in his thigh. Kori ran to her.

Promus looked up at Flicker, defeat glazing his crazed eyes. "Well, don't just stand there like an idiot. Finish me off."

Flicker launched a swift kick to his ass. "I'm not an idiot! I'm not weak in spirit! I do know the righteous from evil!"

"Gimme that thing before you hurt somebody." Kori grabbed the gun from Flicker and sprinted toward the blazing structure, shouting over her shoulder, "Call 911!"

"Back away!" Kori yelled to anyone inside the house who could possibly hear her. She shot the lock off the wrought iron grill and the dead bolt on the front door. She kicked the door open, expecting to see a band of Wheelers clustered in the foyer. Through the smoky haze, she saw no one. Kori dashed around to the back of the house, shot her way in, but found nothing but billowing smoke. She dropped to her hands and knees and crawled down the halfway, opening some of the men's bedrooms. They were vacant. Several explosions sounded from the kitchen. Kori didn't know if they were bombs set there or merely ignited propane. She covered her mouth and nose with her sweatshirt, but she could still feel smoke filling her lungs. Hacking uncontrollably, she rose to her feet and dashed out the back of the building and up to Flicker.

"I called 911. Did you find anybody?"

"No, they must be trapped upstairs. Where's a ladder?"

"In the barn!"

As Kori and Flicker dashed in that direction, they heard a fire engine roaring toward Promisedland from the packinghouse. Promus was crawling into the brush like the worm he was, a viscous stream of blood trailing him.

Kori and Flicker carried the ladder to the main house. "Oh, it's so heavy," gasped Flicker.

Kori barely felt the weight. All those bench presses had paid off. She hoisted the ladder and leaned it against the upper balcony. Scurrying upward, she called down to Flicker. "While I check the upstairs bedrooms, you search the bungalows."

Kori shot off the lock of the iron grill over one window, broke the glass with her boot, and climbed inside. It was Rayann Frick and Roberta Mallory's bedroom. The two elderly women lay on their narrow bunks, fully dressed and holding hands across the short space that divided them. They seemed to be asleep, yet before Kori touched them to check their pulses, she knew that they were gone.

Kori flung open as many bedroom doors as she could, knowing there wasn't time to check them all. She found no one else, alive or dead. She exited out the window she had entered and scrambled down the ladder.

Flicker ran up to her. "I didn't find anyone. Did you?"

Kori shook her head. "No one alive."

"Then where is everybody?"

Kori thought of the rooms she had had no time to investigate.

The fire engine advanced toward the blazing structure. The piercing siren halted; the cool morning breeze stirred softly.

Flicker took Kori's hand and squeezed. "Shh! Listen!" She rolled her eyes east of the ranch house.

From a distance, came a faint humming sound. Her pulse was throbbing so loudly within her ears that Kori couldn't trust her own hearing. "What is it?"

The corners of Flicker's mouth turned up. "Singing!"

They sprinted down the path that had led to the bonfire site. Breathlessly they reached the open field, which now contained the pit of cold, gray ash. The Wheel of Fire members were assembled around it, clasping their hands and singing "Praise God from Whom All Blessing Flow" to the tops of the trees. Leading the congregation, wearing his horned-rimmed glasses and Promus's magnificent bejeweled cape, was Stix.

Flicker cupped her hand above her eyes and rose on tiptoe. "Do you think that's everybody? Inner Wheel looks small."

"Hmm. I don't see Scorch or Match. Flame and Ashe aren't here either!"

"The Mercedes!" they exclaimed together.

"I guess Flame and Ashe made their getaway," Kori said. "That is, Sharon and…?"

"Bruce."

"Ashe is a Bruce? I never would've guessed." Kori touched Flicker's elbow. "And I never would've guessed that you would choose me over Promus."

"I really didn't have time to think. It was as if God were guiding my hand."

"I have to ask: did you aim for Promus's junk?"

"I didn't aim at all. I just pointed the gun at him, closed my eyes, and pulled the trigger."

"You closed your eyes?" Kori repeated incredulously. "It's lucky you didn't miss."

Kori figured Flicker was eager to run into the field to take her place in the Wheel of believers. She hugged her. "I guess this is good-bye for now."

"Wait, Kori," said Chelsea. "Could you give me a lift to the bus station? I need to get back home to check on my mom."

Chapter Twenty-Three

Many of the details of the staged Armageddon came out in court when Vincent Dower, aka Promus, stood trial for fifty-seven counts of attempted murder. Some of the Wheel members remained loyal to him, claiming he never intended to kill anyone; locking them in the ranch house and setting fire to it was merely Armageddon practice. Wheel member Samuel Jenkins told the media, "Promus is on trial like Jesus before Pontius Pilate."

There was speculation that Dower would plead insanity, but he insisted he was perfectly rational and rejected the offer of a lawyer. Taking the witness stand, he stated, "I commenced Armageddon just as Michael the Archangel commanded me to do, and he takes orders directly from God. It's a godless society we live in. I'm probably the only guy in this room who listens when God speaks."

When Kori was summoned to the witness stand, Promus fixed his black eyes on her in a steely glare. She thought about how he had seemed to have power over her in the past, forcing her to act in ways that now appalled and shamed her. When she first began her testimony, her body trembled and her voice wavered, but as the district attorney continued to question her, her statements grew calm and sure. She was telling the truth, and there was nothing to fear in that.

The most damaging evidence against Dower was in Chelsea Cunningham's testimony. She stated the facts in a detached monotone, her eyes occasionally flitting over Dower, who sat reading a newspaper as if her words didn't matter to him. Out of the witness stand, she sat with her parents and her brother, Jack, and sister-in-law, Melanie, sometimes cradling her infant niece.

Although the court attempted to subpoena Flame and Ashe, aka Sharon Dower and Bruce Woodson, they couldn't be located. Some Wheel members testified that while Flame had distracted Promus with an argument against starting the fire, Ashe had unlocked the back door of the residence and led the Wheel members across the field and over the bluff to the hidden camp of Edward Scuttles, aka Stix, before Ashe himself fled the premises.

One Wheeler stated that she had witnessed Ashe park the Mercedes on the shoulder of Blue Ridge Road earlier that morning. "I saw him lock a briefcase and several canvas duffle bags in the trunk," she testified.

Dower stated that the argument with his wife had ended with her sprinting down the private road minutes before he set fire to the house. "If I had a gun, I would've shot her," he admitted.

By scrutinizing subpoenaed financial accounts of the Church of Wheel of Fire, it was assumed that the briefcase contained approximately four hundred thousand dollars in cash. It was speculated that Flame and Ashe had wanted to escape Wheel of Fire sooner, but it had taken them several years to embezzle that much money. Dower's abandoned Mercedes had been discovered in the long-term parking lot at LAX. In the trunk was a cache of firearms, which Ashe allegedly smuggled out of Promisedland to prevent Promus from using them on his people. Flight records revealed that Sharon Dower and Bruce Woodson had fled to Belize. A private investigator, who had been hired by the Church of Wheel of Fire, was on their trail.

Tragically, Rayann Frick and Roberta Malloy had committed suicide before Ashe could walk them to safety. There was also a third death, Joseph Mattingly, known to Wheel members as Scorch. On the witness stand, Travis Collins, aka Match, stated, "Promus ordered me and Scorch to torch the old packinghouse as a diversion. A diversion of what, we didn't know. We also didn't know the Boyz were cooking up a batch of meth in there." The ensuing explosion killed Mattingly and severely burned Collins.

The trial lasted three weeks, and when it was over, the jury reached their verdict of guilty in only a few hours. Dower was sentenced to life in prison without parole.

"Thank God it's over," Kori told Chelsea as they said good-bye on the courthouse steps. "I'm ready to get on with my life."

"Right," Chelsea said, in the same flat tone she'd used in testifying.

Kori shuffled her feet and sang, "Anything you can do, I can do better," trying to get her to smile.

"Singing on Broadway," Chelsea said disdainfully. "That's sounds so lame now."

"What will you do?"

"I don't know. Jack and Melanie have invited me to move in with them."

"That would be fun, watching baby Chelsea grow up."

"It's hard to find something…" Her voice trailed off.

Something meaningful, Kori knew. Something as vital as Wheel of Fire. "How about finding the right church?"

"It wouldn't be the same."

Kori jutted her lower lip in empathy. "Not as thrilling as fighting Satan in the fires of Armageddon."

Chelsea eyes flashed in consternation. "I can't let go…of him. I've tried visiting him in prison. He refuses to see me."

"Chelsea, you know he tried to—"

"I know. I'm trying to work through detachment with my shrink."

"You will," Kori said firmly.

Chelsea nodded, not at all convincingly. "I might get a job, like at a McDonald's…in Corcoran." Her eyes shifted away. "So I can be near him."

"*Vincent Dower?*"

"Shh!" Chelsea looked nervously over at her family, standing several yards away. "They'll hear you."

Kori did what she had to do to catch up on schoolwork and finish her senior year. Graduation felt anti-climatic. It was just one more hurdle to jump before she could start her new life in college. The day after her graduation, her dad called to congratulate her.

"Now, don't you worry, Kori. I've got plenty saved to pay your tuition and expenses."

"Thanks, Dad. How is everything going with you?"

"I've actually got big news. You're going to have a baby sister!" he blurted.

Kori's surprised herself by not being that broken up. She wished she could be gracious enough to offer her dad congratulations, but she just wasn't feeling it. "Mom's not pregnant," she stated matter-of-factly.

He hesitated. "I know, Kori. Do you remember I spent Christmas with another soldier, Tiffany Eggers?"

"Why didn't you tell me you were in a relationship then?" she retorted stridently.

"I'm sorry, Squirrel, I guess I didn't have the nerve. Don't think that this little one on the way means I love you and Jared less. I'll be coming out to see you this summer. I want you to get to know Tiffany. How does a trip to Tahoe sound?"

It sounded like a nightmare. It made Kori realize how far removed her dad had been from her these past months. She simply replied, "Okay, Dad." They could make alternate plans later.

Donald Lawton's lawyer sent divorce papers to Cindy, with a generous settlement so that she could keep the ranch. Soon after that, Cindy sent Vaughn Dirkman packing.

When it came time to move to Sacramento, Kori was eager to leave Goldhurst behind. She would miss Luke, but they could keep in touch by phone and Skype. The day before she left, while he was giving her trusty old truck an oil change in her driveway, she sneaked up behind him and yanked his red rag out of his back pocket. He turned to her and looked at her so solemnly, she thought something was terribly wrong.

"You're going to need an oil change every three thousand miles," he said.

Kori huffed. "Luke! I'll be back at Thanksgiving. Mostly my truck will be parked in the dorm parking lot."

"You'll lock it, won't you?"

"I swear you care more about this old heap than me!"

He took her into his arms, dangling his hands over her shoulders. "I guess my taking care of your truck is a way of taking care of you."

"I know. Thanks." She brushed the hair from his eyes and kissed him.

Chapter Twenty-Four

Kori walked briskly across the footbridge over the American River, leading into the campus of California State University, Sacramento. She'd been in college for three weeks now and was comfortably settled in. She loved everything about attending Sac State. Her classes were interesting, even those for GE credit. As a criminology major, she was excited to be living in the state capital, where laws were actually made.

"Hey, aren't you in my crim one class?" asked a familiar-looking Hispanic girl, who fell in step with Kori.

"Garson, nine o'clock? I love that class."

"I really like it when he talks about his own experiences as a cop." The girl tensed her brow. "It's a lot of reading, though."

"We could study together. I'm Kori."

"I'd like that. I'm Marisol. I must admit being away at college is a little overwhelming. I come from a little farm town in the Central Valley—McFarland."

"Oh, like the movie!" Kori was reluctant to mention the name of her hometown. Goldhurst had been put on the map for a reason she'd like to forget.

"I love being here, even if it is a little scary. It's good to leave all the small town drama behind."

"Tell me." Kori rolled her eyes.

They reached the down-ramp of the bridge and stepped on campus. Marisol hooked her thumb to the right. "Want to grab a coffee?"

Kori pointed in the opposite direction. "Thanks, but I've got Music Apprec. See you in class." She passed the student union, where rows of booths were set up offering services and activities: credit card applications, voter registration, Young Republications, Campus Crusade for Christ. Representatives were handing out brochures, pens, and other freebies. A young woman handed Kori an orange matchbook with the words, "Armageddon, whose side will you take?"

Kori shook her head tersely. She wasn't pleased to encounter Wheelers at Sac State—her turf. She shoved away the pale hand that held out the matches, muttering, "I don't smoke," and quickened her stride.

"Kori?"

She turned to look at the smiling young woman and the curly-haired man at her side. "Spark? Blaze? Hi!" Upon recognition, her attitude turned friendly. "What are you doing here? After all the bad press Promus got, I would think—"

"We're under new leadership," interrupted Blaze. "Promus was once a man of God, but the sin of pride was his downfall."

"Just like Luther," added Spark.

Kori smiled, remembering their habit of finishing each other's thoughts. "I figured he just went insane."

Blaze whirled his finger at his temple. "Power can do that to a man, but Stix is a true prophet."

Kori flashed on the photo she'd seen of Edward Shuttles in the *LA Times*. He had grown a beard and wore a long muslin robe and sandals, like a Jesus Halloween costume with horned-rimmed glasses. The accompanying article stated that Wheel of Fire was recruiting at colleges, urging their new members to drop out of school and remain on campuses, posing as students to snag more of their peers.

"Stix has made a lot of changes," said Spark.

"Yeah," said Blaze. "The angel commanded him to uphold the sanctity of marriage. He's rebuilding the main residence for singles and an apartment complex for married couples and *families*."

Kori raised her eyebrows. "Families? That is new."

"I was only ten when Promus forced my parents to send me away to be raised by my aunt," said Blaze. "Our relationship is still suffering from it." He patted Spark's abdomen proudly. "We'll be raising our own son."

"Oh, congratulations!" exclaimed Kori. "But isn't the world supposed to end before he's grown?"

"It's true we're in End Time," said Blaze, "but Promus mistakenly reversed the inner digits of the year of Armageddon. Stix predicts that the date isn't until the twenty-second century. We need future generations to perpetuate the Wheel."

"I see." It was certainly convenient to predict the end of the world at a date so distant that the prophet would be dead rather than embarrassed if he were wrong.

"Stix plans to choose a smart, pretty wife from our college recruits to start a family himself," said Blaze.

"No Holy Vessels?" asked Kori.

"Those whores?" Spark's face tensed in a frown. "No way! Stix is celibate like all the other single Wheelers."

"And we can eat what we want now, too," said Blaze. "There's so much good will and happiness in the Wheel, you should give it another chance."

Kori glanced at her watch. "I've got class."

Blaze leaned into her and caught her wrist. "Remember, Kori, how ecstatic you were the night you first received the spirit of St. Michael? You can get that glorious feeling back."

Kori gently, but firmly twisted out of his grasp. "No, thanks. I'd rather think for myself."

Spark's eyes popped. "Which Commandment is that?"

"Nowhere in the Bible does it say to think for yourself," added Blaze. "Trust in God, Kori."

She began walking backward, continuing toward the music building. She tapped her head as she called back to them, "God gave me a brain. I'm using it!" She turned on her heel and happily moved forward.